M000223936

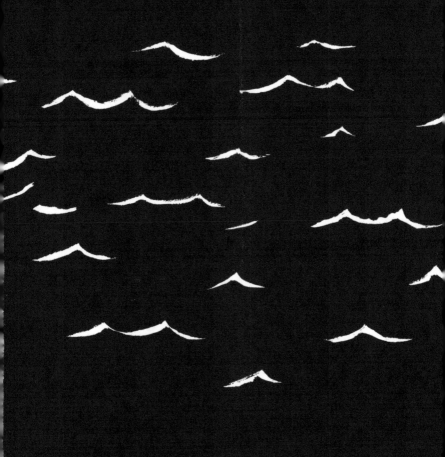

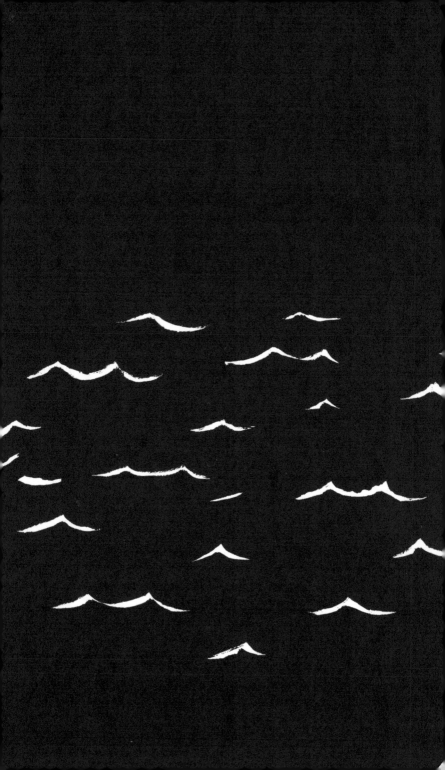

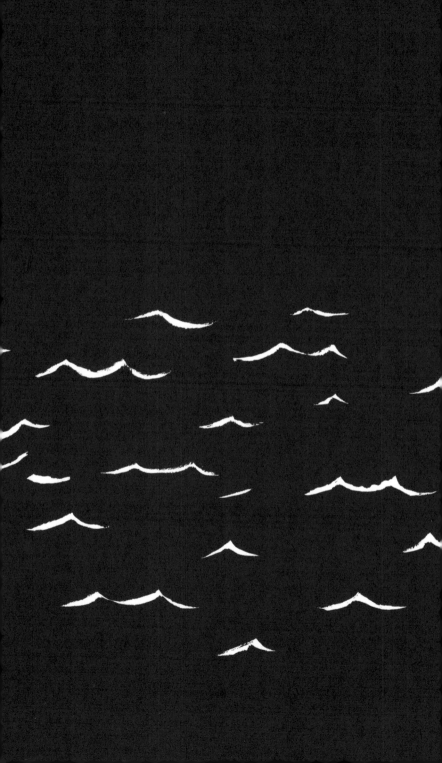

SALMON

SALMON

Sebastian Castillo

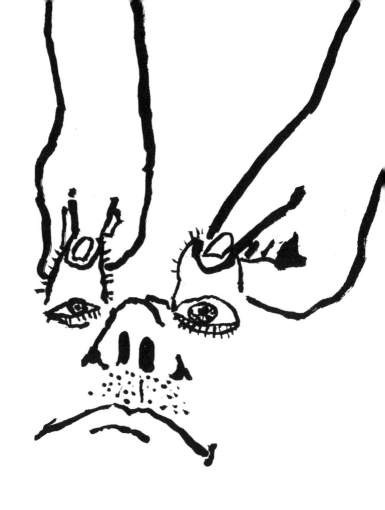

Illustrated by Kit Schluter

First published by Shabby Doll House
May 2023
www.shabbydollhouse.com
@shabbydollhouse

SALMON

Cover and interior artwork by Kit Schluter
Typeset by Giacomo Pope
Set in Adobe Caslon Pro

ISBN: 978-1-7379242-4-1

Dedicated to the good people of SALMON

DRAMATIS PERSONAE

Poet
Boss
Father
Mother
One-Toothed Odd Job
Sleeping Man
Grandfather Eating Soup
Homeless Orphan
Three Junkers of SALMON
Sebastian
Pig Breeder
Ronald
Albert
Local Chef
Golden Boy
Driver
Grocer
Disgraced Wizard
Elector of SALMON
Forewoman
Metallurgist Without Flute
Ruddy Gang of Children
Leather
Portraits of Clara
Alphonse

PART ONE: The world

"You need a village, if only for the pleasure of leaving it."

—Cesare Pavese, *The Moon and the Bonfires*

Why I decided to go to SALMON

My resolve was simple: to say no to the dailiness of life. I would travel to SALMON, where I would be servant, steward, and teacher for a period of one year in their public schools.

Having finished my formal education, I was excited to enter into the world of adulthood, which had always seemed the necessary ornament to place upon my tree. Yes, I would commit to a work, tantamount to adultness itself, and be granted the foremost pleasures of civilization: money, wasting in errant purchases, bathing in regalia.

I was to be a great and handsome poet—a bard who extolled the virtues of the natural world, which includes everything, and is modern always. It is unknowable to those who do not practice verse. Lords, presidents, and prime ministers would invite me to recite lines to their relieved citizens, fanning themselves in large audiences and thanking me for allowing them to see reality.

But my life had not flowered according to that program! No, if I share a story within these pages, it is a record of how my resolve proved inadequate in the face of the world's cheerlessness. It had other plans, and of these contingencies I had no choice but to abide. Yes, simplicity offends no one, and clarity pleases all. I am not aberrant on this head, either in my disposition or character. But my path had crisscrossed with the very spirit of disruption that seems to so fervently penetrate our age.

I had imagined that I would be a lion tamer, and the words on the page my lion. With certainty I can say the whole aspect of what follows is indeed a circus, but I was a mere child in the tent audience, licking a lolli dropped on the grubby earth.

My tenure surrendered

My employer was the first to know of my departure. I had been working at a local wine cellar for several months. Despite my education in natural philosophy, and the commitment I had shown to it, I was not afforded the positions I sought while awaiting the publication of my first manuscript. I was and am a capable formal thinker, though one with the requisite sensitivity to submit myself to poetry. Yes, my mind is endowed with that fine bifurcation: I can fashion numbers and congenital facts into all manner of proper arrangements, and afterward sink deeply into a single feeling, hewing close to that origin of understanding we call natural beauty.

While I had submitted several applications to a variety of august research facilities in our nation, I was greeted with all but silence. Embarrassing my pedigree, I applied to our local zoo's gift shop. When I arrived at that interview, I informed the manager that despite my lack of professional experience, my encyclopedic knowledge of the lives of various fauna would alone prove my performance commendable. I left the shop as I entered it: alone, fingering the dust in my trouser pockets.

This tally of failures reached its terminus when I began my tenure at the wine cellar. I worked in the shop's small basement, which could barely contain the alcohol always in large supply. My primary duty was to arrange the boxes of wine in as efficient a manner as possible. I'm ashamed to say that while I did ply my trade, so to speak, it was merely the trade of having a human body that could hold boxes, and place them where they were meant to go.

On that last day, having completed my usual tasks in the basement with some difficulty, I approached my boss to inform him of my life to come in SALMON. He was sitting where he always sat, at the back of the store, in a decrepit nook he liked to call his *officer's station*. There he had set up an ancient computer, where he would often play video games that had fallen out of fashion before I was born. These games he would play with his hook—that is, the metal prosthetic he used for his right arm, which he had lost in the war. He said he opted for this hook rather than a typical prosthetic for reasons of safety—one never knew when a vagabond might enter the wine cellar with an untoward demand. The truth was that a violent incident had not occurred in that neighborhood for at least a decade, when the two Russell boys staged a mock feud that ended their family line. At the park down the street stood a statue of the brothers hugging to commemorate filial loss.

I told my boss that it was my last shift; I would be leaving for SALMON by boat the next morning. Yes, it is uncouth to depart suddenly from one's station of employment—I would not be able to use this man as some source to attest to my professional character. But I could not be bothered with such decorum and consideration, so ready was I to prove my scholarly mettle in a faraway country.

"Incredibly stupid," he said in response, scratching the top of his balding head with his hook. What I said must have irritated him, for he perforated the skin, and a thin rivet of blood sank down to his forehead. "I suppose there's nothing I can do to stop you. Fill your life with nonsense."

He reached for a bottle of wine that was sitting underneath his desk. It was covered in dust, and a splotch of blood dribbled from his face onto the wine label.

"For you," he said. "A parting gift."

"Thank you," I said. "I'll cherish it."

On my walk home, I walked past that statue of the Russell brothers in their philadelphic embrace. It seemed our city had all but forgotten it, for even in the late dusk light I could see it thinly splattered with animal discharge. There was no one else about. For reasons I could ascribe only to a haphazard impulse, I threw my celebratory bottle of wine into the air—caked in refuse much like the statue—whereupon it rotated pendulously high above it, and later came crashing down on the marble brothers, their heads accented with bits of glass and red wine, which, from my vantage point, and because I had just witnessed the sight of such a thing, appeared to me like blood.

They largely disapprove

I refused to tell my few friends and relatives of my coming departure. I feared it would, through gossip and secrecy, return to my parents. If I had given them even a day to mull over these plans of mine, they would have threatened to lock me in my room.

My parents did not commit themselves to such treasured professional pursuits (my father was a secretary; my mother, a secretary), but they had nevertheless earned a decent life for themselves, and lived comfortably. Part of my resolve emerged from the guilt I felt living off their retirement fund. The wine cellar paid poorly, and by the end of the week I always needed for mother or father to open their purse and slip me coin.

My father dedicated much of his time to taxidermy. He had always argued that the problem with the day's youth were not issues of work ethic or morals, but a lack of hobbies. He suggested that if the youth were to pay greater attention to their hobbies—whether that be the building of ships in bottles, gardening, or sports betting—then their problems would vanish just as quickly. While I was devoted to my empirical studies, and to my work as a poet, I obtained no such leisurely practices. Father did not consider verse a hobby proper.

My mother spent much of her day reading romantic novels: novels where people who should not love each other, due to some accident or other, did, and for that reason a plot could be concocted at great length. Father deemed this an acceptable fashion to pass one's days. Perhaps it's due to this tacit harmony that they've been able to remain together for as long as they have. My mother is in her late seventies, my father even older. After the death of their sole daughter, I was adopted as a consolation prize for their grief and newfound misery. I was merely an infant then, so I do not recall the life of an orphan, though I have felt that shadow plague me throughout my life.

At dinner that evening I announced my plans. I wanted to prove to them that I was taking matters into my own hands, that after years of dejection and confusion, I was to be the author of my own life. I should not like to be written by someone else.

As expected, they both thought I was invoking a bit of mirth at the table. But then, accepting with some trouble the reality of my coming departure, they asked: who will take care of us? Though yes, they are strong in spirit, their bodies grow frailer by the day. A strong gust could be enough to fell one of the two over. Thankfully they did not go out of doors often. As it was, they had most of their requirements delivered to them: their food-stuffs, their medicines, their slight pleasures—alcohol, pipe tobacco, the local rag. I was delivery boy of them all.

"Moreover," my father said, "we shall be lonely. With whom shall we sup?"

"I've arranged for your loneliness, father. The neighborhood boy, whom I have induced after far-reaching deliberation, will not only perform the standard delivery duties, but will join you for dinner as well. Father, he has a stamp collection."

This latter bit was an outright lie, and as I had planned, it visibly quelled my father's unease. He drummed his knuckles on the tabletop. Yes: the image of stamps gathered in a prepossessing volume was visible through my father's very forehead. Mother was not as easily satisfied.

"That boy smells of seawater, something seawaterlike," she said.

"We live inland, mother," I said. "The only water about us is what comes from our taps, and in the sewers below. You must be confusing him with one of those foolish characters in your novels."

"He reeks of ocean!" she shouted, and all three of us fell to silence. I would tell the boy to shower before visiting. To be true, I did not know where he lived, and he was often smeared with some kind of ash, particles of a mysterious nature. He was known as the local odd job, both for the services he provided around our city, and for his bearing. He had but a single tooth in his mouth, and I heard by way of our local butcher that he used it deftly. My parents would be safe.

Before falling asleep that evening, I heard a light rap on my bedroom door. It was mother.

"And what will you be doing there? At this esoteric fish country?" she asked. Our dinner had ended curtly—first with a dismissal of my resolve, followed by a quiet acceptance of that which my parents had no power to change.

"I will be teaching mathematics, mother," I said, lying in bed, duvet covering me from toe to forehead, unable to feel sleep within my body, as was usually the case. She shut the door without saying goodnight.

I had not heard of SALMON until coming across the advert for their government-sponsored teaching grant. I discovered, searching the internet, that it is a newer country, one of the many small nations that cropped up in the fallout of that great war. In its creation, SALMON's constituents had the old order removed. Or I should say, rather, terminated. A great fire was built in SALMON's capital, and those old guard officials—who were, I had read, responsible for horripilating violence—were marched into that fire. The new regime had wished to eradicate any connection to their former nation's past, and in doing so, create a fresh spirit of conviviality and unity. This grant program was one of the many government-funded proposals which assayed such beneficent aims.

Fortunately for me, their requirements were rather lax: all one needed was proof of education, a valid passport, and a burning desire (ha) to acquaint oneself with the people and culture of

SALMON. The truth was I did not know what I would be teaching; I had lied to my mother, though not because I wished to be deceitful. I felt that if I had admitted, along with my abrupt announcement of my departure, that I did not even know what I would be doing at SALMON, I would give the impression that I had not put much thought into my own life.

In the morning, I awoke and gave my father and mother a kiss on their foreheads. They were both still in bed, though not asleep. They wouldn't rise till I had brought them their morning repast: strong, black coffee on the weekdays; a mild tea with milk on the weekends. Though neither worked any longer, they felt it important to retain those habits fomented in their working lives. Without these habits, they thought, they would turn to nothing, and fast.

"Son," my father said, coffee stains dotting his collar. "I was doing some research on this SALMON. I find it odd that this nation's name is rendered in capital letters. Is that a common feature in that part of the world?"

"No," I said, "it does not appear to be general. Perhaps it was an aesthetic choice."

"Your father was saying earlier that salmon don't even congregate in their waters. They are without the fish from which they are named. That I don't like," my mother said.

"Surely they had a good reason to name it so," I said, "celebratory, even. Perhaps they felt the need to honor those humble fish, who so often go without much common regard."

They were building a case against me, yes, even at the moment of my departure, and I needed to present my will as stone-faced, unflappable. It had decided for me, and I could only obey.

"It is only for a year," I said.

"We will live too much alone," said my father.

The doorbell rang. It was the boy. At the door, he appeared well groomed, wearing a clean, white shirt that emphasized his broad-shouldered make. I showed him inside and went over his basic duties, which I had already covered extensively in our inaugural meeting down by the park; I wanted to ensure my parents would receive the best possible treatment. When I brought him to their bedroom to make introductions, both my parents laid there with their four eyelids shut. Neither ever napped, and it was still morning. They were faking sleep! I shook them, and neither budged. Out of desperation, or perhaps embarrassment, I laid atop my father's body, and attempted to pry his eyelids open, which he resisted—essentially proving this was a mere performance, one last petulant, albeit silent, cry of resistance put forth to humiliate me. My father's eyes began to water, likely from the pressure I was applying to his face; I did not (or could not) believe they were tears flowing from sincerity. I was disappointed my parents had resorted to chicanery.

The one-toothed boy stood there dumbly throughout this theater.

"Fine eyelids your father has," he said. "Strong folds."

Bathing in sweat and not knowing what else to say, I agreed, and awkwardly crafted a little speech about how my parents indeed had wonderful eyelids, for eyes themselves are only as useful as the flaps of skin which allow them to breathe freely.

The boy nodded noncommittally and asked for his first payment. I unloaded a sum from the family vault into his hands. The three of us—mother, father, and myself—would have no other recourse but to trust him.

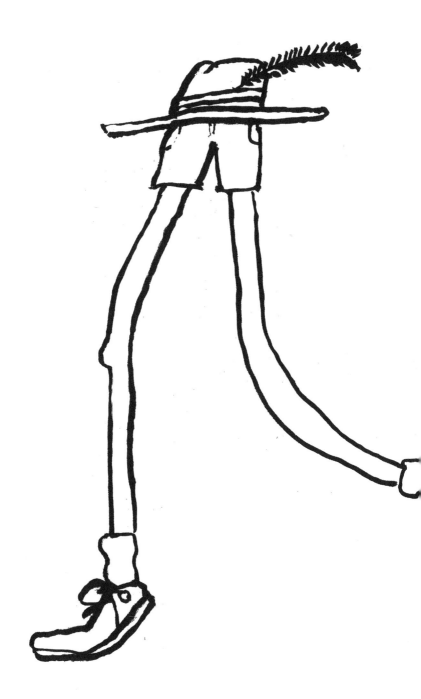

The importance of my satchel

The neighborhood streets that morning seemed to pronounce a certain blankness. While these streets would often suggest utility, a mere loading screen between life at my house and life at work, they now appeared in an entirely different character. The buildings, the boutiques, the damaged sidewalks: all were translated into a foreign language entirely. The very sky above my head—a mustard-sodium glare mingled with leaky-faucet brown—spoke a language whose speech-sounds were foreign utterances, the noise of an ancient child to my ears.

I left the house without saying goodbye. If my mother and father wanted to play a daffy game so let them, but I would not be the one to regret it. I had not mentioned I would be given a break during the holidays where it would be possible to return home to see them—*that* I would leave as a surprise, and my hope was with this surprise would come apology and supplication from them.

With me I carried the clothes on my body and my leather satchel, which held a few, scant items. For years, I've told whomever would listen that this satchel was lucky: it was left to me by my birth mother at the orphanage, the sole item in this world which both of our hands had touched. She embroidered my initials on the inside of the front flap, and instructed the head nurse that in the event I were adopted, the prospective parents must take with them this satchel, with its fine European stitching, and camel-bright tone. I would say to whomever would listen, in fact, that I was brought out of that orphanage sitting *within* the satchel itself. My father strode out of that facility with me strapped on his back, my infant self playing with the few hairs he had left on his pale head. And that, moreover, this satchel was a symbol of my recovery from utter doom, desolation, and lonesomeness: that while my mother did have to give me up, for reason I'll never know, she understood that the possession of this satchel was tantamount to my success.

Yes, all this might sound terribly convincing, an origin myth as good as any, but it simply isn't true. I found this satchel as a child, at school, in an empty classroom. It did indeed have my initials stitched on the inside of the back flap, but likely belonged to a classmate with whom I was not acquainted, who happened to have the same initials as me. I merely brought it home and stuffed it under my bed, where it sat for years. Once I switched to a new school, out came the satchel and the story, which, if not strictly true, is certainly true in spirit. My mother and father never questioned me regarding its sudden existence.

What I had always found remarkable, however, was the glaring, irreconcilable detail I had left within this story, my origin myth, which not a single person had ever once pointed out: my name is an adoptive name; which is to say, the surname of my adoptive father. How could I possibly have the same initials as an orphan baby as I do now? It is my theory, sadly, that people do not listen when you are speaking to them. You might utter a strange, moving, unique detail of your life, and to them, it is as if you had made a passing remark about the weather. One could say: I have always felt a phantom noose about my neck, and all my life I have stood upon a poorly made pupil's chair, ready for it to break into pieces. And if one has said that, if one has revealed such a thing so blankly to an interlocutor, that same interlocutor would hear: nice about this sun we're having, isn't it?

Inside that satchel was a pen, a notebook, few clothes (mostly clergy surplices—liturgical vestments are the shirt of poets, after all), and ninety sleeping pills. I suffer from insomnia.

The shape of salmon

I had never before ridden on a train. Of course, I had read about them in books, and even seen pictures and videos of trains on my computer. I have no mechanical interest, and they therefore meant little to me. Besides: I am but a nature poet, and a student of the natural world. If trains were to offer me anything, it would be through their windows, where I could configure the shape of naturalness in a new and speedier light. I was excited to witness trees and shrubbery rushing past me as I had not seen before.

The voyage to the coast would take approximately five hours. From there, I would board the late-afternoon schooner and be on my watery way. This was all arranged by the grant committee at SALMON, though the literature they sent to me was rather vague in its finer details. I expected the voyage on boat to last a few days, though I was unsure, once I had landed on those fine shores, where I was to go, or with whom I was to meet. I expected a gentleman waiting for me on the docks, holding a placard displaying my name, though as far as I knew, no such arrangements existed.

The passenger cart where I settled was surprisingly empty, and perhaps due to my anxiousness—feeling the morning bile rising up my throat—I found it difficult to pass the time satisfactorily. Much of the train voyage progressed through urban districts in various degrees of dereliction, and as such offered very little of the natural world to enjoy. Once in a while the train would emerge upon a heath, and I could spot some plane trees in the distance, or some unpleasant species of hare running away from its persecutors. But as soon as I was able to get my bearings of that scene, the tracks would re-acquaint themselves with another portrait of vast, concrete emptiness. The world was mostly parking lot, I feared.

I fiddled with my phone, acquainting myself with some of the common foods and customs found in and throughout SALMON. I tried reading an old novel I had snuck from my mother's shelves (I never read fiction—disgusting). I tried, for the first time in my life, meditating. None of it was any use to me! The sole other passenger in my cart was a man wrapped in a tan, gabardine coat, who was apparently reading the paper, but who had fallen asleep while doing so, as it covered half his face, the drool from his mouth soaking the newsprint into a black, syrupy mass. I approached him with the hope of mutually enjoying some traveler's chat, as I imagined that custom was likely typical in voyages such as these.

"One could say this train is not a train," I said, "but a fish." I raised my hands before me and rotated them back and forth, pantomiming fins. "Yes, a salmon, in fact. And these tracks are but a stream —the shape of this train is the shape of that fish, pursuing its goal. We shall fornicate greatly in distant waters. I hope we shall not encounter any roving bears along our comely flow!"

I smiled at him and clasped my fin-palms together. The paper fell from his face to his chest and his eyes opened like that of an emaciated grizzly awakening from his long slumber. He appeared first bemused and then irritated. My attempt at traveler's merrymaking had failed. I explained, hastily, my face growing purple, the purpose of my voyage. How I was beginning my new life in SALMON, and how the shape of that fish had merged with my consciousness—how the world itself appeared to me as a fish, as it were.

"I've barely heard of such a place," he said. "Those new, small countries all look the same, and they're all the same. I'm not even sure I'm remembering the right one. Either way, there's nothing to do there. Most people choose not to live in those places for a reason. And those who do grow bored and die."

"The novelty of change is enough to assuage even the greatest boredom," I protested, feeling as if he were, in the early stages of committing myself to an important cause, mocking my resolution. He didn't seem convinced, no, and I attributed that to his own moral failures in life—failures obscure to me, though which I was sure were multiple and depressing.

A swimmer perishes

It seemed others on board had the same idea as me, for the lunch cart was bustling. There in the middle was stationed a bar of sorts, with a service man dressed in a suit, crimson cummerbund, and bowtie. I took a seat next to a grandfatherly figure. The items offered on menu were pricier than my purse could accommodate, so I settled for some black tea and oyster crackers, as the latter was free of charge.

The old man sat silently beside me, concentrated as he was on his victuals. Some seconds later I noticed a solitary beetle on the face of our dining counter—it must have found its way on board, and was trundling along with a determined, robust gait. It inched towards his soup, and without the grandfather noticing, I watched as the beetle climbed up the side of the bowl and perched itself on the rim. It perhaps fancied itself a bit of a swimmer, gazing down at the soupstuff. *I wouldn't mind a bit of that!*, the beetle had thought. And then by dint of its own foolish pursuit of pleasure, had actually dove into the puree, and killed itself, boiled to disintegration by liquid allium.

"A beetle has ruined my soup..." the grandfather said to himself, his voice cracking.

The beetle floated on the skim of the soup surface, where bits of the milk fat congealed. I inched closer to him, and offered to finish his soup if he did not wish to continue as it was.

"I am already in possession of soup crackers, you see, and I've but eaten an orphan's share this morning," I said. "With which, strictly, I could say I have been acquainted, though in the fog of my memory I see only meals both plentiful and appetizing."

The old man morosely slid the soup across the counter and let me have at it. I figured a bug that had made its way onto this esteemed craft would have to be one of a more noble class, a trusted scout sent here on behalf of his kin, and in that way, I felt it right to sanctify his sacrifice with consumption. The beetle's life would not be given in vain, and with a quiet prayer, I handled the bowl on both sides, and tipped its contents back down my throat, protein and vegetable blessing my empty stomach.

Back at my seat, freshly satisfied, I endeavored to write the first poem of my voyage, and felt that this beetle, now safely ensconced within me, was a fitting subject: a hero who, while explicitly experiencing a real defeat—death by liquefied vegetable—was now to be transformed and immortalized via the sorcery of line and verse into a personage of great importance. I imagined the small fellow nested in pieces throughout the coil of my digestive tract, and eventually deposited en route to that stalwart country, where I would finally be able to complete my first manuscript: written at night, by candlelight, after a toilsome day of teaching school children. Perhaps I would dedicate the poem to him, his sacrifice having not only given me the necessary material sustenance to continue, but also granting a certain spiritual kindness which would encourage the words from my cranium to the pen.

Before I could commit a line to paper, the train cart door opened, and in entered a small boy, dressed in rags. It was as if this boy were the very spirit of wretchedness—a cancerous cell-mass drifting through the aisle of the train. He was accompanied by a necrotic vapor: the odor of shit, piss, and infection.

"Chance you can spare a loose note for an old boy down on his luck, my good bumpkin?" he asked me, holding out a rusted coffee tin filled with dirty coins and costume jewelry. I admit, with some shame, that I felt so put upon, so utterly ruined by the mere sight of this child, that I offered him neither a yes nor a no, and instead turned my head, whereupon I fixed my gaze on the train window. Outside, I could see we were passing a city worker urinating in a public rubbish bin.

The three Junkers of SALMON

Having been so overwhelmed by this peasant child, and with the prospect of my beetle poem, I must have put too much stress on my system, for I fell asleep with pen in hand before writing a single word. Upon waking, I could see my notebook lay half folded on the empty seat next to me, and that my pen was gone, slipping from my fingers in that sleep, having likely rolled down the cart somewhere. However, this was not what concerned me upon waking, but what lay outside the train window: twilight. I had fallen asleep for almost the entire day. More strange, still, was that the train was not moving. I was to board the boat to SALMON in the late-afternoon—and now I had clearly missed that appointment.

We were stopped on a flat, empty plain, though one could spot a small hillock cresting over the horizon in the far distance. Outside, there was a gathering of people about a bonfire, and emitting from that gathering were jeers and paroxysms. My compartment was also empty—the sleeping man from before had perhaps joined the throng outside, or had moved to a different cart with a more comfortable couchette.

Poking my head out the window I could see, at the head of the train, the conductor and engineer apparently arguing over some matter regarding the train's performance. Those gathered around the fire were themselves passengers of the train, and given the size of the fire, it was fair to assume the train had been stopped for quite some while. There were about nine or ten of them. As I walked closer to that fire, I discerned the cause of all that yelling: the small crowd surrounded two boys, both shirtless, fighting each other. One of them was the peasant child from earlier. I had thought this originated from an organic dispute, but upon closer inspection, I could see both boys were in full pugilist costume: oversized, brown gloves; bulbous plastic headgear; loose-fitting nylon shorts each sporting a flag of sorts. There was even an ersatz referee, a man of about my age whom I recognized from the station. The boys circled each other—both their legs jittery but nimble—and each strike engendered the blow of a whistle by the referee. I stood next to three middle-aged men of a similar comportment. After the whistle sounded, one of them would throw coins into a pile, while another removed some for himself. This process—the blows, the whistle, the jostling for money—repeated six or seven times. I was not, however, able to discern the rules governing the game. I did not understand which kind of blow signified some greater or lesser advantage, or who was betting on what. In fact, it felt completely random. The emaciated blond boy struck the peasant boy's jaw twice in a row: each blow separated by a whistle and then a pause. After the first hit, one of the three men grab a handful of coins from the ever-growing pile. A moment later, after an identical movement, the same man would curse loudly and spit at the dirt floor, throwing those recently retrieved coins back into that same pile.

I asked one of those men to explain this game to me, but he remained silent, too concentrated on the fighting's outcome to entertain me.

"I hope this kind of fare is not commonplace in SALMON," I said, "otherwise I can't imagine I'd find my bearings too easily."

Perhaps I had made the appropriate comment, for the man looked over at me and offered a feeble smile.

"Yes, this type of game is common enough at SALMON. It ruins me," he said.

"Ruining all of us," the other said. "My wife and children barely let me leave the house. This is the only action I get."

"Look at us," the third said, "three Junkers of SALMON, reduced to hiding our little habit from those whom we love, only able to engage our delights in private."

I was thrilled to encounter representatives of that country. I could tell they were from elsewhere given their accents, though whether "Junker" designated an honorific or a professional title was beyond me. I did learn, through stilted conversation, that they each worked in the same governmental department in the capital, where I, too, was headed. The fattest of the three assured me there was to be a midnight ship departing, and that if we were to make it to the port town before then, we'd be on our way to SALMON just fine.

"We are three Junkers of SALMON," the first said, "the country where they say they love you, but they fuck you to death."

"They will fuck you to death there, at that country," said the second.

The third Junker played with the few remaining coins huddled in his lap. The fight had since finished, and we could hear the conductor hailing us back to the train, having repaired whatever it was that stalled us so.

The third Junker said: "Before, it was a different place. We three are from different countries originally, you see. We belonged to different lands. Then, after the war... We find ourselves working in the same office, it's true. To your foreign ears, it might sound like we all speak the same language. I'll assure you we don't. We have trouble understanding each other. I'll yell something to *him*, who will pass the message to *the other*, and by the time the response to that question gets back to *me*, it's as if I had asked something completely different, and am receiving an answer to a question I didn't ask. It's all the same to me. That's how we pass the time there. You try to do as little as you can with as much effort as you can muster. If you don't pass the time at SALMON, they will find a way to fuck you to death."

"Sure enough they will," said the first or second Junker, though by that point I had stopped listening, so excited was I to return to my carriage, and continue our sally.

Back on the train I got on all fours and crawled up and down the aisle like a new kind of animal, hoping to locate my pen.

I spent the remainder of my time on that train drawing little pictures in my notebook—of frogs, oxen, and other monsters. I expected the port city to be grand, astir: a hub of exchange and culture endemic to places where people from opposing corners meet out in the open air to speak the custom of their native lands. To my surprise, it looked more or less like my hometown. There were a few more stores, a moribund port motel, but beyond these additions, nothing had struck me as very distinct from the soil and pavement where I had lived my life entire. Unless one counts, of course, the ocean: there it lay, gray and listless in the damp night air. Like the train, it was the first of its kind I had seen in person, and it looked to me like a picture of itself.

The Junker was correct—a ship for SALMON sat waiting for the coming midnight, when it would set off. I presented my ticket and credentials to the schooner's usher, a boy younger than me with a face massively destroyed by acne scars. He half-inspected my items, nodded, and noted my room number—given the voyage would last a few days, I was given the privacy of a cabin. It was Spartan, certainly: a bunk bed and a desk, both of which were bolted to the flooring, I assumed in case we hit rough water. I placed my satchel underneath the bottom bunk and lay down. I was barely tired, as I had already slept for most of my day on the train, and the sound of the ship's engine was deafening: it was as if a mechanical beast were reading to itself the story of its life in the next room over.

It was then, in the first minutes of staring at the mattress above me I realized I was laying in a bed that was not Clara's—that is, my bed, the same bed where my parent's daughter, Clara, had once slept. My parents had never removed any of Clara's effects from her room, even after adopting me, as I grew from tyke to young man. When I was old enough to question the persistance of these objects—pictures and teddy bears and ballet slippers—I was told by them that under no circumstances was I to remove these objects from the room, or throw them in a closet. They said to me that while their only daughter was gone, they felt it necessary to retain a part of her in their daily lives, and this way they could peer into Clara's room each day, and be reminded of their lost daughter. I was not allowed to regale Clara's room with objects and effects of my own. Given that this had always been the case throughout my life, it did not strike me with the force of a lack, though I knew it was not typical. Perhaps it is for that reason—my inability to hang up posters and the like—that I turned to poetry. There, in the space of a stanza, I had the freedom to inject a great deal of pageantry and personality without interference. No one had yet read it, true, but that would not be the case for very long.

I would have to bear Clara's room no longer. Indeed, I could banish the very presence of this girl from my life. It had always felt to me that I shared everything with a phantom sister: my parents set a plate out for her at dinner, and heaped food on this plate, where it would remain uneaten and grow cold. When I would ask to select the radio program that we would listen to in the evenings, my parents would turn to the empty chair next to the three of us and ask the absent Clara whether or not she agreed with my selection, and the answer would inevitably be no. They would say: Clara doesn't want to listen to that, sorry. So instead of listening to my favorite arboreal program, they would submit me to an hour of the most anodyne game show about pop culture from twenty years prior. I learned things like: there was once a great singer who died tragically, from drugs or a plane accident, or both; an award-winning movie everyone loved wasn't so good after all; that owner of famous race horses was in fact murdered by a stampede of those same horses, so zealously devoted were they to their sport.

Here I was in my own room—though, yes, temporary, my own nonetheless. I welcomed the buzz of overloud machinery, the chirping of mice and insect in the schooner walls, the antiseptic scent floating in the air. At the very least I had a lock on my door.

Who is he?

After a few further moments of idleness and reflection, ensconced there in the private commode of my thinking, the door began to jiggle against its frame. The being on the other side did this at first politely, and then with greater animal force. I found myself yelling: it was occupied, clearly! At last I heard the slide of a key into the keyhole, and the door opened wide. I felt, within me, a momentary whisper of horror: there stood a man, and he looked exactly like I did. That, at least, was my impression. The same did not seem to register on his face.

"It appears we'll be lodging here together," he said. "My name is Sebastian."

"I didn't know there would be another," I said. "Mmm, I'm sorry, but—I really do need my privacy. I simply cannot sleep if I hear the undulation of someone else's breath. Poets require a poet's solitude, after all. You'll have to find a room elsewhere."

Sebastian smiled and nodded uncomprehendingly, as if I had spoken to him a foreign language he was supposed to have learned at school, but didn't. He placed his duffle bag on the desk and with a vulgar athleticism jumped to the top bunk, skipping the feeble plastic ladder intended for that very ascent. The mattress above me sunk considerably, so that his bottom was only about a foot or so away from my nose. We lay silently for a moment.

He said he was going to SALMON, too. What was more: he was to become a teacher there under the guidance of the same government program responsible for my own voyage. We discussed our deeper motivations for travel, and I told him of my difficulties in finding work suitable to my tastes and interests.

"Yes, for a period of some months I've worked as a secretary at a reputable lawyer's office," I lied. "And while I've learned a great deal about the laws of our nation, it felt entirely too minor a vocation for me, something better left to smaller minds, minds entertained by the frivolous and arbitrary wills of judges and their clerks. My parents were secretaries."

"I don't know much about the wills of judges and clerks," Sebastian said. "Their lot appears to me a tall order. I've been working as a stock boy in a liquor store. Moving boxes and so forth."

As he was speaking, his face pointing downwardly at me from the top bunk, I could not help but notice even greater similarities between the two of us. While he styled his hair a bit differently, his mannerisms mimicked my own. I thought, perhaps, this was merely a generational inheritance. After all, when one watches a film from a bygone era, there is a moment of rupture when one hears its personages speak: certainly they share a language with the present, but it's not our language, it's not our rhythm, our cadence and timbre. So while Sebastian did in fact resemble me quite a bit (though I believed I was the more attractive), this further coincidence of our speech and mannerisms was nothing more than the coincidence of having been born at more or less the same time and place.

I shared with him the slight disturbances of my day: the trouble with the train, and how I had slept by accident, which was unusual for me. I feared I would have to take one of my sleeping pills that evening. Often, when I am unable to sleep, it is as if there are voices roving through me, each with their own troubles and concerns, and each speaking more quickly than the one before. They mount both in pitch and volume, and I find I can barely lie in bed. These, of course, are the voices of the dead, and as such, the voices that create the possibility for the writing of poetry. One must be their antennae. For this reason, I am wont to take a midnight stroll, notebook and sharpened pencil in hand.

"I've never had that problem," he said. "In fact, my entire life has been plagued with its opposite. I fall asleep far too easily. I can fall asleep standing. I've fallen asleep at parties, at weddings, and even, if you'll pardon me, at funerals. All I have to do is say to myself: I am becoming a sleeper. And the day has ended for me."

I thought he was exaggerating for comedy's sake—wanting to bridge the social distance between his temporary flat mate—but within a few seconds, I could in fact hear him sleeping. I inspected him: a thin rope of drool hung from his mouth to his chin hairs. I clambered off my cot. Feeling somewhat fatherly, I laid a blanket on top of Sebastian and turned off the desk lamp, letting a sleeper get at his work in proper conditions.

Meetings with an estimable pig

I wandered aft, though not by choice: I tried to make it to the bow, to peer out onto the horizon as we sailed to meet it, but I was rebuffed. A guard at the end of a hallway, decked in authoritarian belts and chains, informed me that passengers were not allowed beyond the point where he stood, and moreover, were not allowed to make the most cursory contact with the captain and his mates, for matters, he explained at length, having to do with boating insurance, which I would never in a million years, he added, understand. I was told to go play elsewhere.

At the stern of the schooner I happened upon a handsome scene: the fat Junker (jolliest of the three, and visibly drunk) consorting with a woman of middle age, dressed as if she were on her way to the ball. Next to her, a black pig on a leash, bleating softly. They were seated on canvas chairs, gazing up at the twin moons, which hung above us in cloudless splendor. Though there hovered a slight chill on deck, the air was still, and offered a pleasant atmosphere for a late-night chin wag. It felt to me like I was entering the penultimate scene of some moral fable. I sat in the empty chair next to them, and began nodding, as if already understanding the stream of conversation which I entered in stealth.

"No. He's beyond that," the woman said, "he's simply… Oh! He's on another level entirely…"

The Junker nodded and made cooing noises, apparently directed at the pig.

"Alphonse comes from our most esteemed line of hog," she continued. "You could not ask for a more advanced darling. He's able to trace the faintest fragrance. *Put that which you seek in the midst of a heap, and Alphonse will speak.* My father came up with that tune. Yes, well, he died recently, unfortunately. In an accident. Everyone is dying of mere accidents now. Whereas I remember when disease used to be all the rage."

Meekly yet full of wonder, I reached out to pet the pig, Alphonse, I presumed, and the woman in retaliation yanked at his lead quite harshly, pulling poor Alphonse closer to her, away from my reach.

The hog let out a high-pitched squeal, though soon recovered, it seemed, for he was oinking privately yet again within a few seconds.

"Please ask next time you lay yourself on my dear. He's worth more than the sum of your life's wages. I don't wish to assume perfidy on behalf of all who seek to avail themselves of darling Alphonse, but one mustn't be too careful."

"I'm awfully sorry, ma'am," said I. "But the temptation was too much to bear. Your boy is inviting, certainly."

"Certainly, he is," said the Junker, blinking violently.

She introduced herself as the heiress to an elite pig breeding commercial enterprise, though pigs used not for consumption or other plebeian diversions, she was quick to add, but for the professional tracking of rare and costly mushrooms: truffles, exotic varieties of caterpillar fungus, and others of psychoactive comportment. In the latter category, of which Alphonse was a specialist, were mushrooms with heteroclite, experimental properties. Indeed, mushroom which, if ingested, can make one entirely conformist in nature, stripped of identity or individual thought: a mere lemming who will do what they are told. Or alternatively, mushrooms which can transform one into a pure and simple weapon. These mushrooms are as dangerous as they are rare—at the moment, she added, there were people in the world dedicated to synthetically replicating their genetic structure for the purposes of war and interrogation. To get one's hands on the organic originals would be to put oneself in a position of great financial influence.

"And these mushrooms, they're common in SALMON?" I asked.

"I don't know and am uninterested in the goings-on of that nation," she said. "I'm loaning Alphonse to the royal family for a small fortune. They want to perform some kind of experiment. He'll be running in a maze and a poor scientist will have to write down how Alphonse manages. I find it risible, but one needs money."

"Risible, yes," the Junker said, "but one can bear risible for a risible price!"

"Yes, risible," I repeated, not quite knowing quite what I was saying, though feeling that by repeating the words presented to me I would somehow count these two as peers, or more importantly, they would feel the same toward me.

"May I pet the exquisite Alphonse?" I asked.

"Thank you for asking formally! No! My boy has had a tumultuous day of travel. He needs time for himself, away from touch and admiration. Don't we all at times."

I peered down at him and the pig's gaze met mine. The light of the two moons had formed a Venn Diagram on deck, and Alphonse sat in its center, the common ground between two celestial arguments, it seemed.

The apparatus of mathematics assumes a mysterious purpose

The days at sea spread out without purpose or punctuation. I spent most of my time wandering the deck, occasionally meeting with Sebastian for coffee in the mess. We would sit across from each other, mumbling something or other regarding the day's weather, which thankfully was often calm and cloudless. I would nod at him, mentioning the calm, cloudless quality of the day, and he would nod back, accepting the calm, cloudless quality of the day. He would say something to the effect of: Nature is on our side, my good poet. And I would say: Impossible. And he would say: Sure, why not.

The crew and captain remained spectral as ever. Apparently, this was a precautionary measure due to the presence of Alphonse. Given his worth, the captain thought it best to deny contact between those working the ship and its passengers, for fear that certain passengers, catching whiff of the precious cargo held aboard, might think something rash and foment a mutiny. One of the Junkers had told us this over breakfast, the rumor spreading aboard. It felt preposterous—prohibitive, foolish. As it was, the vessel was sparsely attended. Beside me, Sebastian, the Junkers, and the pig breeder, I could count at most another seven or eight passengers. The crew must have outnumbered us by a fair margin.

One morning, something emerged on the horizon: a cargo ship. Colorful containers dotted its side, each a tidy square, as if the ship were a pointillist canvas. If one squinted enough, one would have been able to make out the shape of the famous "smiley face" on the ship's side. I mentioned this to Sebastian, as we were both standing starboard, gazing at the fast approaching ship, but he said he couldn't make out any pattern at all. Despite the fact that he and I exchanged only a few words on our days aboard, we were spending more time together, as if feeling listless in someone else's company was preferable than to list alone.

It was then for the first time we saw who we presumed to be the captain of our schooner. She was standing on the level above us, and given our position, we could make her whole countenance, though she could not see us. The captain was tall and extremely thin, and wore a thick, black turtleneck. She looked to me like a mime, or some sort or experimental performer, the kind of which was more or less common in my hometown's central square. These performers would often throw a dizzying number of balls into the air without managing to drop a single one. I feared and admired them, and I found those feelings projected then onto the captain. She held a phone to her ear, and grumbled something assenting. She asked for the party on the other line to meet her in the hold in three hours' time.

Now, I am not one for gossip or meddling in the affairs of others, that is true, but given the general veiled spirit aboard, Sebastian and I decided it would not harm anyone if we happened to peek around the hold when that time came. The excessive mystery of our condition aboard piqued a child-like curiosity within us.

Back at the mess later in the afternoon, we sat with two new companions, both of whom were mates on the cargo ship, which now floated parallel to our own. These men were gruff, yes, but their diction and locution were impeccable, as if they were politicians who had decided to rough it before dedicating themselves to their futile political careers. As it turned out, they were musicians— Ronald and Albert—who had taken on seasonal seaman's work to fund their band's existence.

"We have quite the system in play," said Albert, rotating several of the rings on his middle finger as he spoke.

"System is the word for it: the four of us band members devised a strategy using the vast apparatus of mathematics in our service," Ronald followed.

"To what end?" asked Sebastian, who seemed genuinely curious. I was making conversation to be polite.

"Each of us are paupers," continued Ronald.

"We are but paupers," said Albert.

"Nothing in our pockets, not a nickel in our coffers," said Ronald. "But our love for what we do —my love, Albert's love, and the unyielding love of the two others—was nickel enough to keep us at it."

"Two of us work together at sea for half the year," Albert said, "and the two who remain behind write the music."

"Then, we switch places. They work at sea, and we write the music. This way," said Ronald, sentimentally, "we can afford our lives: our instruments and recording sessions and practice spaces. We haven't been in the same room for years, but we've made great progress."

As they were speaking, their faces were so close together that their cheeks pressed upon the other's. They paused, waiting for our verdict.

"Oh," Sebastian said, "what fun. That sounds very elegant."

"Yes, whichever felicity suits you," I said, though I didn't mean it, and feared I was missing some essential understanding of their enterprise. No, I was not marked by confusion—why anyone decided to organize themselves the way these sailors had is their business. But it seemed their program existed only for its own sake, to prove it worked. Their argument had left me feeling I understood the world less by a minor, though noticeable percentage.

Wine-dark sea change

It is here I must confess I committed an error of some magnitude. For all my life, the ambivalent decisions I've made throughout the day have always led to the same results: the morning sun rises at the edge of my window, and I go about my habits.

After our long lunch with the musicians, Sebastian and I made our way to the ship's hold, which required us to sneak past a sentry, for this was not an area of the ship where passengers were permitted. Our curiosity was not so great, or abetted by any deep spirit of longing. It was merely the product of boredom, which is so often a wellspring for mischief. In the hold there sat large casks of wine, larger than a man—at least fifty, each labelled with their variety and vintage. As I was telling Sebastian about one of the Spanish riojas— I don't drink, no, but a poet must know their wine —the hold door opened and in walked a besotted throng: ten of the cargo ship's crew members, including the musicians, a shifty red-headed figure who in the course of the coming conversation identified himself as the other ship's captain. Lastly our own captain entered, and under her arm, somehow, Alphonse the pig. Sebastian and I hid behind one of the casks.

It became evident this rendezvous at sea was predetermined, and not innocent in character. The cargo ship's crew received Alphonse; our captain received payment from the redheaded captain; the musicians laughed all the while, pointing at the various casks of wine. The captain gestured in the direction where Sebastian and I had been crouching, and informed the cargo ship's crew they were free to take a number of barrels as a consummate tip for this transaction of theirs. Everyone but a few of those crew members left through the hold's only door, and it was then I felt the hum of panic course through me. If we made a dash for it—it would be made obvious, if not now, eventually, that we had witnessed the entire scene, along with the robbery of this precious pig. I did not want to think of what would come of us then.

I opened the puncheon we stood behind and, to my surprise, found it was half empty. Sebastian and I jumped in, and sealed ourselves within it, soaking in wine up to our breasts. I felt a cold trickle throughout all my zones, the grape-dark syrup entered our holes and pockets. As luck would have it, two cargo crew members hoisted this very same wooden drum onto a dolly and we were transformed from passengers to accidental shipment.

Never were I to think I would have to narrate my life with head and hands in a stock, and yet that is precisely where my foolishness had brought me. It is no surprise we were soon discovered. Pirates are thirsty, after all. Those endless, stultifying days at sea, where so often one has so little do. Why not drink? Why not have a spot of something, tip it back, and let it dance amid one's brainstem? Yes, that's what these vagabond sailors must think to themselves all the live-long day. I don't blame them. Whoever you are: I would rather see you drowsed and world-stupid than witness you suffer through afternoon boredom.

We were regarded as stowaways, and I suppose strictly speaking, we were. No trial, no jury, of course. Sebastian and I were first castigated for spoiling a cask of wine. Then, it seemed, these pirates realized they faced a far greater problem: we knew about their pig. Without a moment to explain or protest, they dragged us to the stern of the ship, and chained us to our station. Perhaps this feature of their boat existed for instructional purposes, even to the crew: one did not want to end up there, did they, and alighting one's eyes upon those stocks was enough to remind one to behave. Even pirates must have their rules.

Above us, the gulls swirled. Or, I had imagined, as I could only hear them, my head firmly in place in my wooden stock. O, birds and their plangent calls—yes, their nasty bird-speak, directed at me, proudly shrieking that whatever befell me did not admit the courtesy of human speech, that the rest of my life would be filled with noise indeed, and that I had already heard the last words I would hear, for ever more.

"I'm going to shit all over myself," Sebastian said. "I haven't shat in days. I have stomach problems. And I get that traveler's constipation. But now I'm ready to unload fiercely."

Sebastian called over one of the pirates, one who had spoon fed us some slop earlier, and he admitted Sebastian to the head, where he shat at gun point. Which, if not ideal, was at least considerate.

"What do you think they'll do with us?" I asked, once Sebastian had returned, emptied sufficiently.

"They'll have a beauty pageant, of course," Sebastian said. "Yes, they'll provide us with some swimming costumes and the judges will determine which of the two of us is the sexier."

It shames me to say, but having realized the likely outcome of our stay with these men, I began to weep. I had not wept in many years. In fact, the last time was when I was first told by my parents that I was not their blood-born child, that I was bought, essentially, from the orphanage store, and that they could have picked any other child at random, but that it was in fact me whom they chose, not because I fit any pedigree, but because it had simply been that way. Yes, that was the last of my weeping—I let it all out, as they say, back then, and once I was done, I had sworn I would not cry for the rest of my life. That I would put the days of crying behind me.

"Maybe we can reason with them," said Sebastian, conciliatory. "Convince them they can buy our silence about the pig with our lives. My silences are exquisite. I don't care what they do with the pig, that's the truth. Though I do enjoy that portly fellow. The way he walks."

It was the truth for me as well, and I agreed.

Our friend, Alphonse

Alphonse, possibly knowing the peril and likely doom he had cast upon us, began sleeping in front of our stocks, as if, in some way, he was trying to let us know he was sorry. It was a mystery to Sebastian and me why this precious cargo—indeed so precious that we had been imprisoned for merely knowing he existed—was allowed to wander the ship so. He was a billion-dollar pig, no? And here he was, strutting about the place freely! And what's worse, not only did he strut, wander, scuttle, what have you, but he had also very much developed an adversarial relationship to a certain demonic monkey who lived aboard. And the pirates allowed this monkey to terrorize poor Alphonse.

The monkey, who was only ever called "monkey," belonged to the ship's chef. This man, referred to by everyone as merely "the local chef," wore a Tyrolean hat of sorts—much too small for his head, as if he had stolen it jestingly from his toddler child, and was now wearing it in order to play an unknowing dunce for the satisfaction of this same child. Adults do this frequently enough in front of their children. He was always shirtless. The chef had the longest nipples I had ever seen in my life. They looked like over-large eraser heads jutting out of backside of dual pencils, which must have sunk into his chest. I passed on this observation to Sebastian—why would a man need erasers for nipples?

"To correct the many mistakes he was to make in life," Sebastian said glumly.

The chef passed by, monkey on his shoulder, and whispered something to his private primate. The monkey then leapt heroically off the chef and landed squarely on the hog's rump, shimmying up to his back and pulling the pig's ears as if he were commanding a race horse. And poor Alphonse squealed horribly—I mean truly, horribly. Never had I heard such discomfort communicated from the mouth of a non-human creature. The monkey drove the pig around in a drunken figure eight pattern before us.

"Ride that little money pig bastard!" the chef bellowed, and then gesturing at us, said. "I'm giving you boys a show at least. Must be dull out here all day."

"We could use some sunscreen," Sebastian said a bit brattily, to which the chef replied with a low whistle, and the monkey, looking up from his mischief, leapt from the pig, back onto the chef's shoulders, and then, needing no other direction, pounced on Sebastian's head and ripped out a chunk of his hair. Sebastian, maybe wishing to retain a little dignity, remained silent. I would not have been able to do the same. The chef and the monkey went off elsewhere.

It was then that Alphonse, having recovered from his humiliation at the hands of the demonic monkey, waddled over to Sebastian, and licked lightly at his feet. I should, at this stage, simply come out and say it: I felt a great fondness, no, a kinship to the pig. Its two eyes were like my own eyes. The immobile mask of the pig's face was my own. Its four limbs were like mine. It's black, dapper fur—well, perhaps not. I am not so hirsute myself. Alphonse nestled himself between us and fell asleep. To the north, a flock of birds flew in a tight circle: a spinning grey halo over the ocean water, or maybe, the earth itself.

*The pirates offer us no certainties and we
meet a violent, wholly baffling end*

There was, it seemed, an open question on board
as to what they were to do with us. Or really, a
series of grunts and whispers. Were we to be
thrown off the side of the ship, feasted upon by the
eager, pre-historic beings below? Dropped off at
the next port with a few billfolds in our pockets?
Blinded, beaten, gagged, and raped? It was clear
we needed a summit with that red-headed captain,
who still had not deigned us with his presence.
Sebastian and I both felt that, given our more am-
icable than not repartee, Ronald and Albert, the
pirate-musicians, were perhaps our best hope in
gaining an audience in good faith. Surely, artists
such as themselves would have a soft spot for a
poet down on his luck! As for Sebastian, the subject of art had, surprisingly, never presented itself
in conversation between us.

"Our dear fellow," said I, when the opportun-
ity struck—near us, Ronald was dumping a bucket

of urine into the ocean. "How we need your help my good bard!"

"Oh, the twins," Ronald said, I suppose in reference to the nearness of my appearance to Sebastian. "Sorry about all this. Well, not really. Not my decision, after all."

"We'd like to speak to the captain," Sebastian said. "We want nothing to do with you, or with any of your sick crew dealings. I am sorry for my rude behavior but I can no longer feel my neck skin, you see, and I've been nearly trepanned by that monkey creature."

"Not at all," said Albert, coming up the rear, carrying another bucket of urine, or really, I don't know—some thick liquid. "We don't hold it against you. You both look awful. Could use some sunscreen. But you did spoil a decent cask of wine. They might kill you. They might even roast you alive and eat you. We really have no say. We're paid for our work here on ship, then we go back home. Pirates have no common goodwill among each other."

I could not believe it—I had thought, at first, their anger regarding the wine was simply a pretext for the much bigger issue of our knowledge regarding their pig thievery. They were, in fact, punishing us because of the spoiled Spanish rioja! They didn't care about what we had witnessed—or they didn't know we knew about Alphonse's true worth.

"Yeah," Ronald said. "Yeah, they were pretty angry about that. We're out here for so long. Every drop is precious, really. Last year we had a fellow who drank beyond his share. You don't want to know what they did to him."

"What did they do to him?" asked Sebastian.

"They blinded, beat, gagged, and raped him," said Albert. "No, no they just fired him. But they were really very cruel about it. Quite cruel, yes. It was untoward."

He was cut off by screaming near the bow. Both Albert and Roland turned their heads and the sheer bewilderment of their expression struck fear within me.

"The sail is gone!" Albert said.

Sebastian angled his head, peered upward, and gasped. He repeated what Albert had said. And then—it is difficult to accept this, yes, but accept it you must—*the stocks disappeared*. Both Sebastian and I were freed. I blinked my eyes, and they were gone, as if reality had swallowed them whole. At the bow, we heard a thunderous crash—the stocks reappeared hundreds of feet above the ship, in the middle of the air, and fell downwards on to the deck, smashing themselves and whatever lay underneath them to bits. The same then occurred with the vanished sail, though a hundred feet away, over the birds who were still flying near us in the shape of a halo. Now the sail hung above those birds, draped over their circumference, so that a canvas platform floated in the air above the ocean, a portable theater stage built by the birding class of natural life.

Shouts and confusion reigned over the scene. It seemed that the ship, for reasons entirely unaccountable, was simply vanishing from the physical world. It was as if we were displayed on a computer screen, and some malevolent deity sat behind that same screen, pointing and clicking at objects they wanted to remove. The ship's ivory wheel—so massive that only a giant, or a man on a ladder, could to use the device—had vanished, though I could see not where it reappeared, if anywhere. The shouting and prayers ascended to an ungainly pitch. After all, disaster is so often incongruous with any rational account for how one's hours are supposed to render themselves.

The entire ship would be next, and we would drown. Then, the world would transform into that darkness known only to deep water. I was certain it was to be my end. Every thought from that realization till then would be a thought toward my grave. Sebastian stood somewhat morosely, as if this were not a surprising result at all, but another bit of theater that one must endure, whether its results would be an eternal blank, paradise itself, or something heretofore unknown to the daydreams of men on earth. I felt, oddly, at that moment, that I wanted to live a life worthy of biography. Yes, just then, on the edge of what was certain to be the event horizon of my own voidhood: a book about me for someone to read. That wouldn't be too much to ask. A biography that was as short as possible, with only the good bits.

PART TWO: The island

"The tiny little fish enjoy themselves
in the sea.
Quick little splinters of life,
their little lives are fun to them
in the sea."

—D.H. Lawrence, "Little Fish"

Poet awakes inside a thatched hut. Empty bottles surround him. Across from him a boy sits at work at his desk. Behind Poet, an overly ornamental wall sconce holds a large candle, whose flame is bright and spritely. Every two or three seconds the sconce and candle disappear and then reappear a few feet to the left. The cumulative effect is that the large room is lit from each angle of the hut within the span of half a minute, counter-clockwise.

POET (clutching sheet): How now! I lived.

GOLDEN BOY (screwing a bottle shut): And how. Yes. We recovered you from the shore.

POET: A tragedy befell me.

GOLDEN BOY: I would not imagine otherwise. Your clothes were in tatters, and we took you for dead. But a pulse I did feel. Father and I dragged you to our hut here, which we dedicate to our work.

POET: To what do you dedicate yourselves?

GOLDEN BOY: We bottle the island's alcohol, and prepare it for distribution. We come from generations of this sort of work: men of the bottle, though teetotalers us all.

POET: How strange.

GOLDEN BOY: It isn't true, either, but saying so grants us a kind of whimsy from afar. We're alcoholics.

POET: You are but a child!

GOLDEN BOY: Old enough, as is. Are you not curious about the candle?

POET: Heavens yes. How scary. We do not have that from where I come.

GOLDEN BOY: They don't have this anywhere. Other than here. It started up again a few days ago. Seasonal tick.

POET: A vanishing candle tick?

GOLDEN BOY: No. On this island grows some manner of fungus whose principle effect is what you see.

POET: To move candles about?

GOLDEN BOY: Nay. To disappear and reappear objects, and all manner of dead and inorganic things. The other day we found father's bicycle at the top of a palm tree. Here we just call them trees. But for your sake: a palm tree. We had to ask those awful children over to help fish it out. A proper ordeal, that was, and it delayed deliveries to boot.

POET: Of the alcohol.

GOLDEN BOY: Liquid goofing itself.

POET (coquettishly): I once worked in that trade...

GOLDEN BOY (pausing his work and pointing something sharp): That's nice.

The front door opens, and enters a man, short, dressed half as a gentleman, half as a tramp: a rather sharp sports coat up top, time-battered basketball shorts down beneath. He walks with a limp, though perhaps for effect.

GOLDEN BOY (advertising erudition): Hallo mein Father.

DRIVER: Ho! You up, then? Been close to half a fortnight.

POET: Your son was introducing me to island life, as it were.

DRIVER: Best to get used to it. Hold on to your knickers and all that.

POET: Oh, but what a tragedy befell me. Yes, what a tragedy. How I hope some of my companions shared my luck!

DRIVER (the pleasure of redaction in his voice): Perhaps they did, and you'll find out soon enough. The island is small indeed. Much of it is inhabited sparsely. There's the big town. Then, of course, there's the little town... Otherwise you have pockets. We inhabit one such pocket, though it's one of the most spacious on the island, given the importance of our work.

POET: You are bottlers. Bottlers of alcohol. Importance is but relative to one's needs, indeed.

GOLDEN BOY: Shall we bring him to Leather?

DRIVER: Soon enough, soon enough! We still have work today. Young man, you will help us. What with the fungal disappearances and us tending to you, we are behind with our urgencies.

POET: I really must be going. I was en route to the nation of SALMON, where I shall be servant, steward, and teacher for a period of one year in its public schools. Having finished my formal education, you see, I was excited to enter into the world of adulthood, which had always seemed the necessary ornament to place upon my tree. Yes, I would commit to a work, tantamount to adultness itself, and... well anyway, I'd imagine I'm already late for my orientation and such.

DRIVER: You must forget that. You must let go of such a thing.

POET (hotly, then regretting his tone): I think not.

GOLDEN BOY: It's not so bad here. We play card games when the weather calls for it. And all the drink you'd like.

POET (doing something really annoying with his face): I don't drink.

DRIVER: That's fine. But yes, we can address your questions and pleadings at a later time, when you meet Leather. He's the man of the island, as they say.

A fierce pounding on the door. Someone is yelling and cursing outside.

DRIVE: Come in, blast it.

A woman of middle age kicks in the door so forcefully it slams against the hut walls, shaking the foundation of the lapidary structure. The mounted sconce candle falls to the floor and is extinguished. She has the proportions of a body builder, but it's more so genetic than habitual.

GROCER: Late!

DRIVER: Barge of a woman.

GOLDEN BOY: Our visitor is up finally.

GROCER (with the affect of a Prussian censor): And where you from?

POET: Elsewhere. That matters not. I was en route to SALMON, as I was telling these fine bottlers, and I'm keen to continue my trip thereabouts. Can you direct me to the island port?

GROCER: Island port!

Golden Boy and Driver laugh.

GROCER: Island port! Next he'll ask where we keep the caviar vending machines and virtual reality sex parlor.

POET: You must have a port? A place to dock your vehicles?

DRIVER: Nay. No port. Sorry kid.

POET: But how did you lot end up here?

GOLDEN BOY: We smashed upon the island we did!

POET: What? Smashed?

GROCER: Can I borrow him? They need an extra hand over abouts the distillery.

DRIVER: I certainly don't own him.

GOLDEN BOY: I'm growing fond of the boy's deportment, though, so do return him.

POET: I woke up but five minutes ago! I don't even know whose clothes I'm wearing! You are but a child!

DRIVER: Mine, from mine early youth. You're welcome to keep them. Had them in the closet in the case I lost my late-onset adolescent weight. But my case is useless. I've grown much too accustomed to how I behave to make any differences in my life.

GOLDEN BOY (whispering): My father is inclined to a charitable disposition, you see. It's how I've acquired my far-ranging bonafides, for which of course I'm endlessly thankful, remote as we live. When you return, I'll show you my *calculation notebooks* which I've committed to idiosyncratic thought.

GROCER: Right. Well, come, come young man! I need a virile specimen such as yourself, only for a few hours or so. I'll give you a lolli as a treat. Come!

Sebastian and Disgraced Wizard stand outside a mausoleum. They guard the embalmed corpse of the island's founder. Disgraced Wizard chugs a bottle of wine.

DISGRACED WIZARD: Almost out.

SEBASTIAN: Give me some.

DISGRACED WIZARD: Go check to see if he's still there. Earn your keep.

Sebastian peers into the mausoleum. The corpse has not moved.

SEBASTIAN: Still in his frosty, glass case. Now let's have at the syrup. Your boy needs a little satisfaction. He doesn't work for free.

DISGRACED WIZARD: You're lucky you receive payment at that! You don't know what we've done with the others…

SEBASTIAN: There are no others.

DISGRACED WIZARD: Yes, well, I admit there haven't been many who've come here by accident, that's true. In fact, come to think of it, only one—the metallurgist in the little town. Came in on a paddle boat, if you'll believe it. Said he wanted to leave the earth. About a year ago. It was just him and his dog and his flute. Dog died soon after. An infection of some sort. We carry no veterinarians here, though we do have a nurse. Then he lost his flute. He was quite sad about that...

SEBASTIAN: Never met him. Sad about his dog. A dog is a nice thing. They enjoy your company. I have no comment for the flute.

DISGRACED WIZARD: Well, anyway, out of pity, we just sort of let him hang about town, and his trade was useful enough.

SEBASTIAN: Right.

DISGRACED WIZARD (mawkishly): Here you go.

Disgraced Wizards hands over bottle of wine to Sebastian, who downs the remains in one gulp. He seems somewhat drunk already, at this early morning hour.

DISGRACED WIZARD: He should be here soon. Man's been slower than usual.

SEBASTIAN: And I'm thirsty yet.

DISGRACED WIZARD: Maybe he'll remember to bring us lunch this time.

SEBASTIAN: What's on the menu today?

DISGRACED WIZARD: Fish.

Driver pedals his bike around the corner. He produces a chime sound with the bell on his handlebars. His Tyrolean hat disappears then reappears on his balding head as he approaches.

DRIVER: Boys!

DISGRACED WIZARD and SEBASTIAN (like infants): Hello.

DRIVER: What's the move today?

SEBASTIAN: Guarding the corpse again.

DRIVER: The present is for duty, as they say. Rest comes later.

DISGRACED WIZARD: It looks like it's what we'll be doing for a while. The fungus is putting us to work.

DRIVER: Well, it's a tale as old as the island, isn't it.

DISGRACED WIZARD: Sure.

SEBASTIAN: We found his body at the foot of the volcano yesterday. Took us three hours to figure out where he was.

DRIVER: That must have been a hike, no? Carrying the old geezer back all that way?

DISGRACED WIZARD (gestures faux-sexually): Look at the muscle on him! It didn't take so long once we found him.

SEBASTIAN: I was pretty drunk the whole time. I don't really remember. Speaking of which!

DRIVER: Yes, yes.

Driver removes a number of bottles from his satchel.

DISGRACED WIZARD: From God's urethra to our mouths.

All present drink.

DRIVER: Do you fancy my new hat?

DISGRACED WIZARD (speaking with an indescribable accent): And from where did you get it?

DRIVER: Found it washed up on the shore, of course, of which I've taken the wont to calling "the world store."

The hat has, throughout this interaction, appeared on the heads of all three men, as if playing a children's game. None of the present company seem to care or notice.

SEBASTIAN: We're hungry.

DRIVER: Ah, but I brought you a loaf today! Yes, a prime loaf. My son has been baking some of that stately German Schwarzbrot. The first few loaves were awful. Hard enough to use as bricks.

SEBASTIAN: I'm not picky.

DISGRACED WIZARD: We're not picky, no.

DRIVER: This one is pretty good. Yep. Here, your daily bread.

Driver hands over a loaf of black bread to Sebastian. Sebastian and Disgraced Wizard eat the bread. It tastes terrible. Sebastian and Disgraced Wizard look like martyr-saints before they've been canonized.

SEBASTIAN (through bread): Mighty island cuisine.

DRIVER (embarrassed he has a son): Well, I like it.

Elector of SALMON arrives riding a tandem bicycle. It is pink, covered in bunting, and projects a festive, slightly feminine spirit. He rides the bicycle alone.

ELECTOR OF SALMON: Drinking on the job,
I see. Eating stately German bread on the job,
I see.

DRIVER: I was delivering to them their daily order. Relax, ye cad.

Driver spits at the ground but doesn't have enough
saliva in his mouth, so bits of sputum merely cake
his beard. He wipes it off his chin using his blazer
sleeves, the way children use sleeves to clean their
faces.

ELECTOR OF SALMON: Idiot man!

DRIVER: No need to offer up any report to him.
I was on my way as it was.

ELECTOR OF SALMON: I will write up reports on whomever I please. It is my duty to
deliver him daily reports. I am a deliverer of
reports. I was once an elector, a man given the
task of electing. That is, back then. Now, I am a
man of reports. If I wish to write a report on
you, so be it.

Elector of SALMON spits on the ground successfully. Due to the heat, the saliva evaporates instantly. The Tyrolean hat appears on his head. He grabs at it fussily and casts it to the ground as well.

SEBASTIAN: Any news today good Elector?

ELECTOR OF SALMON: I have told you to never address me directly. You are not of the island. You are remoras. You are a leech. I would spit on you had I saliva left.

Sebastian takes a big gulp of wine and then, tilting his lips upwards, ejects the wine from his mouth in a thin jet.

DISGRACED WIZARD: Look, he's a fountain. We're at the fountain. Let's throw coins at him.

ELECTOR OF SALMON: Filthy fountain! Had I a coin worth less than nothing I would drop one into you all.

DRIVER: Make a wish, Elector.

ELECTOR OF SALMON: I do not believe in
the wishing of anything. I came here to tell
you: Leather has returned from the volcano
coves. Yes, his absence was... Well, I was getting worried, of course... But he has returned
and requests that all of the island be present in
the large town square at the twilight hour. Be
prompt, imbeciles!

Elector of SALMON rides away on his tandem
bicycle. A bit of bunting falls to the ground, which
Driver picks up and drapes around Sebastian.

DRIVER: Do the fountain again.

Sebastian repeats his fountain pantomime. All
present enjoy the performance a second time. The
Tyrolean hat spins upside down overhead, as if an
invisible hand were twirling it on its pointer finger
like a basketball. Sebastian gets some wine inside
the hat.

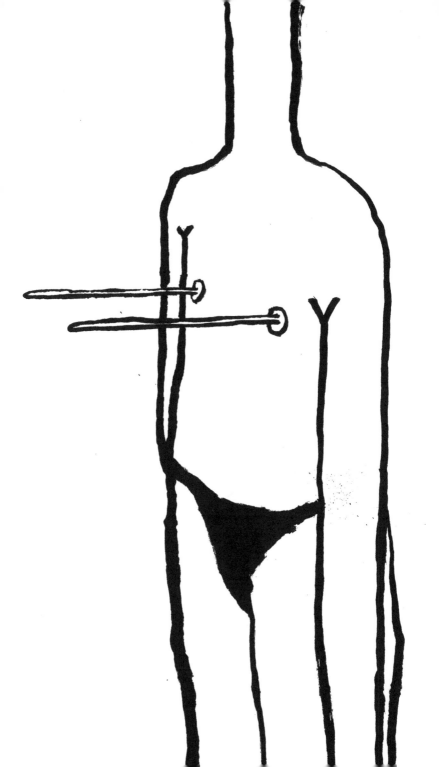

Poet and Grocer enter the island distillery. It is a large compound, with a tremendous vat at its center. Along the lip of the vat are wooden ladders, which men climb and then descend, apparently tending to the fermenting liquid within. The distillery men do not pay attention to Poet and Grocer.

GROCER: A proper nucleus of the island. Without it, we'd go mad.

POET: How lovely.

GROCER: It is. It is lovely, actually. Thank you. Wasn't my idea, of course, that'd be the old man's.

POET: The old man?

GROCER: The founder of our island. God rest his soul.

POET (mock solemn): Yes, yes. What a work he's left behind. A big vat.

GROCER: Just you watch. D'ya not wonder how we make this hooch?

POET: Grapes. I don't know. Island potatoes.

GROCER (smiling how someone would imitate a smile they had seen in a photograph): Go look for yourself.

Poet climbs an unused ladder up to the mouth of the vat. He peers down to the bottom. It is covered in black, volcanic rock. What's more: each of the rocks has a human-appearing mouth it opens and closes. When the mouths open, they release carbonation. The rocks have two bumps where eyes would be but they lack eyelids. They are permanently closed. Poet descends ladder.

POET: My God. Rocks with mouths!

GROCER: Rocks with mouths? Who cares that they have mouths! I have a mouth. Birds and other things have mouths… No. The mouth is not important, but what comes from it. Alcohol!

POET (poet-like): This island is a blight upon the human earth. The result of a demon god who begat without courtesy. I am going to cry…

GROCER: The earth is no more human than it is anything.

POET: And from these little burps they produce alcohol? Why don't you just bottle it here? I don't understand the misted vapor of your island habits.

GROCER: You ask too much. Yes, our founder discovered this. These curious onyx stones strewn about the foot of the volcano. They all give off a slightly sweet scent. And, well, yes, they had mouths that opened and closed. He put some in water, and next thing you know: wasted! It was as if we had all won the lottery. He even stopped looking for the mushrooms for while, if you'll believe it, but that only lasted a few days, mostly because he was drunk.

Forewoman approaches the pair. She's dressed in tatterdemalion rags, though she wears them well. It looks fashionable even. What can one say—she's charming beyond clothing.

FOREWOMAN: Oh! Is this the other one? They look so much alike.

GROCER: Yes. He's finally awoken from his sleep: the long sleep of a little baby, and now we're teaching him to walk. Figured this was the best place to start things.

POET: They? Alike?

FOREWOMAN: That one has really lost his vim since starting here at the island. You look much healthier.

GROCER: Hopefully you'll fare better. That boy does nothing but drink. Which, to be true, doesn't make him very different from most of the men on this island.

POET: Did he tell you his name? Was it Sebastian?

GROCER: I don't know, or maybe I did, and I have forgotten. It doesn't matter to me.

FOREWOMAN: Glad you're here. We just got a delivery of rocks out back and I need a big, strong fellow such as yourself to bring them down into the basement.

POET: I wish to not handle these wretched stones, madam.

FOREWOMAN: They're already in boxes. We have those awful children go scavenging around the foot of the volcano with these boxes. I make them actually. They're pretty good boxes. Anyway, they go around the volcano and they come back with boxes filled with onyx stones. We're a bit behind due to the fungus season. Go on now.

POET: Madam, while I am sure the need to continue with your potion making is urgent, my needs are much greater. I have heard tell that a certain Leather is the man about the island. I wish to meet with him and explain my situation. I shall need to expedite a voyage from this island to the shores of SALMON, or at least thereabout, for I have lost precious time in my endeavors.

Grocer slaps Poet across the face with a thick stick of island bamboo. He keels over, face first, his nose and face now bloody. She hits him once more on the ground for good measure.

GROCER: The woman said get to work, you brat! The other one didn't complain like this.

FOREWOMAN: No, he didn't. Maybe a nip of the good stuff will convince him. That worked for the other.

GROCER: He says he doesn't drink.

POET (in the manner of a weeping supplicant): Yes, I don't drink. I am a poet who breathes through his nostrils, and commits his lonely evenings to verse, or to the dream of verse. Please don't strike me, you ghastly woman. For now: I bleed! I bleed!

Forewoman crouches and mother-wipes Poet's face with a lavender-scented kerchief. It has a short poem about the lives of fish printed on it.

POET: What is this? A poem?

FOREWOMAN: I'll let you play with this kerchief in due time, young man. You have soiled it with your idleness and whatnot. Now, boxes to the basement.

Poet gets to his feet and, with a sullen air, accepts what he must do. A goblin-like man ascends from the basement staircase and approaches the three. He looks cursed.

METALLURGIST WITHOUT FLUTE: Ah, good, good! Yes, good, good. A boy to move the boxes from here to there... Good.

POET (still bleeding): Who is this loathsome creature?

Grocer threatens to hit Poet again, though seeing him wince and make infant-like sounds of awful anticipation, stops short.

FOREWOMAN: You are to report to him.

GROCER: This one needs it all spelled out, doesn't he?

FOREWOMAN: All spelled out, it seems. Can't just do what he must.

POET: I have agreed to the terms set upon me by you. I am merely asking useful questions.

METALLURGIST WITHOUT FLUTE: What's useful will be determined by us, mind you. You will be integrated. I was once integrated. It turned out to be a lovely process. In the basement you will find an array of boxes, each labelled according to the vintage of the stone.

POET (on the verge of tears): Rocks have no vintage!

GROCER: All spelled out for him…

METALLURGIST WITHOUT FLUTE: Indeed, they do here. Everything is multi-factored here, and everything will become transparent and integrated for you. I once had a flute, you see, and I would play the flute to understand the world very easily, but then I lost the flute. Anyway, if those awful children have managed to understand the rock situation, a grown boy such as yourself should have no trouble.

FOREWOMAN: You can tell by the cries they emit from their mouths. If you can't hear anything—they're baby stones.

METALLURGIST WITHOUT FLUTE:

Yes, baby stones to be placed at the far end of the basement. And if you hear a full-throated howl, they are ready for submersion. Place them near the front of the staircase. Simple as!

GROCER: You'll get it. Well, I'll be off. Remember to bring him to Leather's gathering later this afternoon.

METALLURGIST WITHOUT FLUTE:

He has returned?

GROCER: Yes, I passed by that dreadful Elector earlier and he told me so.

METALLURGIST WITHOUT FLUTE:
Despicable man.

FOREWOMAN: I'll say. Anyway, you're on the
clock now, as it were. Boxes!

METALLURGIST WITHOUT FLUTE:
Boxes!

GROCER: Boxes!

Poet is put to work.

Sebastian and Disgraced Wizard stand outside a mausoleum. They guard the embalmed corpse of the island's founder. Sebastian chugs a bottle of wine.

SEBASTIAN: Almost out.

DISGRACED WIZARD: Already?

SEBASTIAN: We kind of went to town today, yeah.

DISGRACED WIZARD: We have gone to town. Graced the village of our pleasure.

SEBASTIAN: The hamlet of our desire: graced, pillaged.

DISGRACED WIZARD: What time is it?

SEBASTIAN (using philosophy): Oh, late afternoon. The time of day I struggle with most, I'd say. Too late to feel one can seize anything, really, but too early to give into an overall feeling of completion. Of having completed an important task. The very thing one should have completed. Do you hear what I mean?

DISGRACED WIZARD: We only have an hour or so left. Then we can head over to the large town. I'd like to have a go at one of those sausages. I hope the sausage vendor is there today. Can you believe that man has a six-pound beard? He says it strengthens his neck.

SEBASTIAN: I do like a fine sausage. Though I can't say it's my favorite food of cylindrical make. It doesn't rate for me.

DISGRACED WIZARD: What's the list?

SEBASTIAN: Banana. Gherkin. The long egg. Varieties of cylinder candy. Only then sausage.

Golden Boy rounds a corner and approaches the mausoleum.

DISGRACED WIZARD: Ah! The good and dutiful son of our fine Driver.

GOLDEN BOY (green around his face): Good day, gentleman.

SEBASTIAN: Nipping your own supply today have you.

GOLDEN BOY (sort of irritated, but not really): As have you, island stranger.

SEBASTIAN: I'm a stranger no more, thank you! I've lived here now a week. Made my stay utilitarian, I'd say. I'm as good as gravy. A proper island lad. I'm integrated. You won't see a faster integration.

DISGRACED WIZARD: Don't get too comfortable. As soon as we lack the work, we'll cast you into the ocean.

GOLDEN BOY: Yes, off to where you came from, the nothingness of water.

SEBASTIAN: Yeah, right. Don't you need me! And don't I know it. Who else but me to help guard the old man's corpse.

DISGRACED WIZARD: Yes. It's been at least an hour. Go check.

SEBASTIAN: Another time. Let's wait till we're almost through here.

GOLDEN BOY: Already shirking his duty!

SEBASTIAN: You're as drunk as I am.

GOLDEN BOY: Yes. This is expected of me, for I am of the island. Not yet a man, but a foal soon to be racehorse.

SEBASTIAN: You weren't born here.

GOLDEN BOY: No, true, but as a mere newborn swaddled in my mother's shawl, I can hardly recall a life elsewhere. My dear mother...

SEBASTIAN: Enough sentiment out of you.

DISGRACED WIZARD: Come now, let the boy indulge his softness.

GOLDEN BOY (wiping tears): No matter... I came here for some help, actually. Half our bottles disappeared.

DISGRACED WIZARD: Half? Are you on a bit of island humor?

GOLDEN BOY: Nay. Half, yeah. I go to relieve myself in the ocean for a tick, turn my back for a tick, as it were, and when I come back, half the bottles gone!

SEBASTIAN: Pity.

GOLDEN BOY: Yes, a pity.

SEBASTIAN: Well, go look for them?

GOLDEN BOY: I have. Found near four or five. But at this rate at least a third will still be missing by nightfall. I need your help.

DISGRACED WIZARD: Sorry boy, we've got a job here to do.

GOLDEN BOY: You're but standing around in the melancholy dusk light!

DISGRACED WIZARD: Important work indeed.

Like a great tumbleweed of human proportion, Ruddy Gang of Children roll onto the scene. They immediately create a sense of great chaos around the mausoleum. Some jump off nearby trees, others foam at the mouth wildly. Some merely stand there, dirty. At least one of them holds a bottle under their armpit.

RUDDY GANG OF CHILDREN: Bottles! Bottles! We want bottles!

GOLDEN BOY (truly furious, like really): You awful children, you! These are property of the island! They do not belong to you!

RUDDY GANG OF CHILDREN (smashing bottles against a stone): Bottles for no one!

Ruddy Gang of Children throw the bottles they have found among themselves as if performing an intricate choreography they have rehearsed before, all the while Golden Boy attempts to snatch them from midair, to no success.

GOLDEN BOY: Brats! Give them!

SEBASTIAN: They're all kind of the same age aren't they?

DISGRACED WIZARD: Yes, but Golden Boy is infinitely more refined. He's read things in Italian, if you can imagine. Ruddy Gang of

Children just go about with their various odors.

SEBASTIAN: Golden Boy, leave them be. I'll help you with your bottle search. They have but a few among them. That Leather will sort them out.

DISGRACED WIZARD: You will do no such thing! You are to remain at your station till I have relieved you. Do not forget that I am your immediate superior.

SEBASTIAN: Why don't you use some of your supposed magic then to help out our dear Golden Boy?

DISGRACED WIZARD: I magic no longer... I have told you. No, that life is behind me...

GOLDEN BOY: Aw, this creep never had any magic in him! That's what my father says.

DISGRACED WIZARD: (assumes a posture of discursive combativeness, though one perforated with insecurity)

GOLDEN BOY (the pleasure of denigration in his voice): He was just another performer. A side show freak. He would let people light him on fire and electrocute him for a few coins. They would put dangerous things on his nipples.

SEBASTIAN (fatherly): Oh, the boy is redirecting his humiliation toward you; I've seen it happen before many times. It's but a human affectation, and he has much to learn yet. I believe in you and your magic.

DISGRACED WIZARD (in a low, pitiful voice, having lost yet again): Go check the mausoleum.

Sebastian walks over to the tomb and peers inside. The founder's corpse has disappeared.

SEBASTIAN: He's gone again…

RUDDY GANG OF CHILDREN (dirty, banging pots and pans somehow): Gone again! At the foot of the volcano! Find him in some stupid hole! Buried finally, and gone for good!

DISGRACED WIZARD: Aw, Christ.

SEBASTIAN: Yeah. Only a little bit till we could have knocked off for the day, too.

GOLDEN BOY (feeling somewhat ashamed for his previous outburst): I can help look.

DISGRACED WIZARD: No, no, my child, you must continue your search for those precious bottles. We are counting on you. I can go look on my own.

SEBASTIAN: Don't be like that. Sheepishness has helped no one escape a day in jail.

DISGRACED WIZARD: No. You go help him, and then head toward the large town. Once you've found a few of those bottles. I can tell Leather about it later, and we'll commence our search bright and early.

RUDDY GANG OF CHILDREN (spiritually foaming): Fuck shit piss! Fuck shit piss! And! And!

GOLDEN BOY (as if sweeping rotted food remains into the garbage): Disgusting varmint!

Off you go, you've caused nothing but harm, poison, and a conceptual bleeding among us today.

Ruddy Gang of Children laugh and amble around the corner, dropping their pots and pans to the ground. A large cloud of dust remains hanging in their wake. All present begin sneezing.

GOLDEN BOY: (sneezes)

DISGRACED WIZARD: (sneezes at an above average intensity)

SEBASTIAN: (sneezes even louder)

DISGRACED WIZARD: (sneezes gauchely)

SEBASTIAN: (sneezes like he's doomed)

GOLDEN BOY: (sneezes like dairy cattle)

Ruddy Gang of Children make various mocking mooing sounds in the distance between their fits of laughter. No one rides by on a bicycle.

A village square in the large town. Off to one side sits an elevated platform, atop of which is a lectern. A speech is soon to be given to the islanders, many of whom listlessly mill about nearby: sailors, vendors, retired slumlords, excommunicated clergy, factory workers, dispossessed artists, chemical engineers, and a few malnourished children. Sebastian and Elector of SALMON stand side by side, facing the lectern, having just arrived on the scene. It is soon to be twilight.

SEBASTIAN: The man himself.

ELECTOR OF SALMON: And you should consider it a privilege.

SEBASTIAN: At every request to meet with him I have been told: You are a speck of shit! I suspected he didn't exist. Not that it matters to me.

ELECTOR OF SALMON: He's a busy man. Yes, a man of plans and their execution.

SEBASTIAN: Just like me. I wake up and my big plan is to go to sleep later.

ELECTOR OF SALMON: You are not a tenth of him. And he himself is not a tenth of our dear founder, gone but not forgotten…

Elector of SALMON begins weeping. The mere suggestion of this man is enough to get him started. Sebastian rubs his back gently, which Elector of SALMON slaps away. Poet, smeared by dirt and sweat, approaches. He looks terrible.

POET: My heavens, Sebastian!

SEBASTIAN: My friend! There you are. You look beleaguered.

POET: I lived!

SEBASTIAN: Yes, I lived, too.

POET (already talking about his problems): They've put me to work on this wretched island, Sebastian.

SEBASTIAN: As they have to me. Can't escape it.

POET: My life is plagued by boxes… Always boxes…

SEBASTIAN: Maybe I can put in a good word for you at the mausoleum. We could use a third man. A mausoleum is like a box you don't have to move.

ELECTOR OF SALMON: Two is already one too many. The young man will remain at his box duty.

POET (with real human desperation in his voice): We must find a way out of here, Sebastian.

SEBASTIAN: Oh, we'll figure something out, or we won't.

ELECTOR OF SALMON: He's here!

A man approaches the lectern. Leather. He's dressed more or less like a cowboy: leather boots and vest, Stetson hat, denim otherwise, though all he dons is cracked, creased, and generally dirty. It is as if he has emerged from a murky, difficult place. His eyes are bloodshot. It looks like he's wearing white face paint. Though he is of medium height, and somewhat frail, his voice is stentorian.

LEATHER: There has been, for a number of years, a variety of rumors regarding the nature of my name. When asked, it is true I do not answer, but merely peer at my interlocutor— peer, I'll admit, with total venom in the manner I hold my face—for I do not like questions being put to me. I do not find a question that is put to me as something pleasing. Least of all do I feel the urge to answer such a question. And in fact, I don't answer, and haven't answered. But the truth is that I do, indeed, finally feel the need to say something is the matter with my name. Something portentous. That is, my name has its origin from superficial and entirely arbitrary designations, like most names, and only later did it take a certain, deeper significance.

Leather pauses. The crowd claps lightly. A sailor pumps his fist in the air as if to suggest a "you tell them"-style camaraderie, though he doesn't understand a word that has been said.

LEATHER: My grandfather was a tanner, or rather, he owned a tannery. He was quite successful. And it was from working with animal parts, I believe, that my own father, our founder, took an interest in the natural world —its flora and fauna—an interest which, many years later, led us to this place. My grandfather was known as Mr. Leather... As such, my father became Little Leather. And privately, between us, at least when I was a child, my father called me Little Leather Junior. A double diminutive. I would never grant someone this degree of implicit condescension other than my father. And even from him—it was simply too much. At a certain stage in my boyhood, I said to him: You will call me Leather. At this, he laughed. If he was Little Leather, how could I be Leather? He didn't accept it. He couldn't. But publicly, that is what I became. It is a way of honoring my grandfather's trade, and our family's relationship to the natural world. A common goodwill exists between those creatures and me. It is to this relationship I attribute much of my past and future successes. But more importantly, it is a name which exists as a testament to my position in the world: I am a man who has never cringed, and who has arranged everything for himself.

The audience has lost some of their initial enthusiasm. They now stand in anticipation of Leather's conclusion. At least half of them think of their forthcoming suppers.

LEATHER: I have asked you to come here for a simple reason: I have found the first of what will be many of the island's mushrooms. Yes, you've heard correctly: they are, finally, ours!

A semi-elated confusion erupts among the crowd. Chatter and clapping. Elector of SALMON weeps.

LEATHER: With these mushrooms in our possession, we will at last be free to promote our wellbeing to the extent to which I have always wished. My father, pure and simple at heart as he was, wanted to cultivate the fungus for, I suppose, reasons that were purely scientific, and therefore egalitarian. I have no such desires.

The sailor from before pumps his fist in the air, this time with a little more confidence.

LEATHER: We will delete those lands responsible for our condemnation! We shall vanish portions of this earth!

The crowd roars. Elector of SALMON is on his knees, still weeping, hands clasped as if in prayer. Poet and Sebastian stand motionless, statue-like.

LEATHER: We will excise nations whole cloth! The fungal deity of the island has been unveiled. It will now work for us. And I am its bargainer!

More cheering. A whatever-you-say-boss attitude runs like a current throughout the island denizens.

Leather steps down from the platform and approaches Elector of SALMON.

LEATHER (afterglow): Good. Reports later. You
and the foreign boys, come.

The sun has set. The twin moons loom overhead.
The dim, nocturnal light shines down over the village square, and the throng disperses, like cockroaches who have been caught in the act of feeding on crumbs.

Inside Leather's domicile—almost a palace, a structure unlike anything else on the island. Despite it's size, his home is a single room. Leather, Sebastian, Poet, and Elector of SALMON sit at its center—a living area. They are surrounded by a large number of marble statues, each in different poses. Some foist a sword into the air above them. Others appear to be cradling a baby (there is no baby). Another statue is posed as if masturbating, though upon closer inspection, they are merely scratching a supposed itch on their genitals. There's a coffee table at the center of the room, atop of which lies the embalmed corpse of the island's founder. All four are drinking tea.

LEATHER: We brought these statues with us when we left our home... They would surely have been destroyed or deposited into the sewers had we not secured them.

ELECTOR OF SALMON (holding back tears): Our founder...

LEATHER (holding large clump of volcanic mushrooms): Yes... I held the fungus betwixt my hands, and I thought very deeply of my father... I thought of how he dressed, and how he stood... I thought, too, of how he sneezed, and how much he disapproved of in our world... Lastly, his face: it was there before the canvas of my mind. And then, something happened, and his body appeared here, right in front of me. This is only the beginning for us.

ELECTOR OF SALMON (openly weeping): Father...

SEBASTIAN: That's quite nice. Learning how to drive them, I suppose. Driver's education, but for the humble extra-dimensional volcanic mushroom.

POET: Where did you find them? I don't understand. Your remarks take a certain mixed aspect.

Elector of SALMON, on his knees, caresses the founder's cold, frozen cheeks. Leather kicks Elector of SALMON in the face.

LEATHER: So, fancy hearing the island legend?

SEBASTIAN: Mmm. I don't care either way. So no. No.

POET: But I do! Yes, legend.

LEATHER: My father, the founder of this island, deceased though forever in our hearts, etcetera, shepherded us here close to a decade ago. We are from that place which you call SALMON, though it had a different name when we all lived there. It could be said that many of us escaped what was a likely fate—the fires in the capital and other such forms of persecution. We landed here because my father had heard, when he was a boy, that on this island there grew fungus with marvelous qualities, and that with this fungus we would be able to pursue remarkable, beneficent things...

POET: How is it possible that an island of such repute was uninhabited?

LEATHER: It was, as they say, a family secret. A map of the island's volcano had been handed down for generations. We were a family of botanists, tanners, mythologists, and scientists. The island is also quite small, of course, and without this foreknowledge, not particularly attractive. And there were tigers...

SEBASTIAN (losing interest): Tigers, really?

LEATHER: Yes, we had to dispose of them.

POET: How many?

LEATHER: About fifty.

SEBASTIAN: How did you kill fifty tigers?

LEATHER: We shot at them with guns. Afterwards, we ran out of bullets, and have fashioned a bit of a pacifist attitude among ourselves, more or less. Among each other, that is. Not towards you or the rest of the world, of course.

SEBASTIAN: Very handsome of you all.

POET (doesn't know why he's asking question): Did you eat the tigers?

LEATHER: They disappeared. It was as if we had unlocked something on the island. As if the tigers were the keepers of the fungus, that is, keeping them from us.

SEBASTIAN: You mean the fungus did its disappearing act on the dead tigers?

LEATHER: One by one the bodies of these tigers would vanish. Then we saw that they would reappear in the sky and come crashing down. They crushed one of us. One of my brothers, actually. The Elector's twin. Death by falling dead tiger. It was as if the fungus were playing with their corpses. Then, the tigers disappeared for good, and we never saw the rest of them. Maybe they were cast into the ocean, or into the volcano. But as my father famously said, "Who cares." He was only concerned with finding the mushrooms and creating a life here.

POET: And you've yet to find them, I presume.

LEATHER: That is correct. Until now.

Alphonse the pig emerges from a darkened corner. He ambles forth reluctantly, but also with a sense of stage purpose, knowing he's being called to present himself, and now must occupy a space in the ongoing amusement.

POET & SEBASTIAN (Christmas morning): Our dear Alphonse!

LEATHER: This little fellow washed ashore, gagging in salt water. Those awful children found him, and, like good little island tykes, alerted me. I suppose they wanted to eat him. But I could discern the pig's pedigree immediately. What surprised me, really, was the extent to which this little fellow excelled. Alphonse, is it. I suppose he was on the same ship as you both? I took him into the cove labyrinth and he guided the way with his precious snout.

Leather delicately taps the top of Alphonse's head with his finger tips, as if trying to extract the pig's brain from its skull. Alphonse releases a guttural tone that sounds like something between assent and ambivalence.

ELECTOR OF SALMON: Brother... let us bring father back to his mausoleum.

LEATHER: Yes, yes, we'll have the boys take care of that.

SEBASTIAN: So Alphonse here is the hero of your little abject feuilleton.

LEATHER: Not quite. I had realized, for all these years, we were mistaken. The map of the volcano was a map of something else: the cove beneath. That is, below the volcano, underground, is an inverted volcano, a byzantine, maze-like network which leads to a deep nadir, which is likely the source of the fungus.

POET (assuming authority): We're pleased for your success, and indeed, the future success of those here on the island. You'd like to take over the world, erase entire nations whole cloth, etcetera. That is none of our business. However, now that we have an audience, we must implore you—we do not belong here, everyone knows this, and we'd like to be granted a passage away from this place.

LEATHER: Yes, perhaps this will be possible. But you must earn this passage.

SEBASTIAN: Why not. Thanks awfully.

LEATHER: The cove is a knotty matter. Alphonse here can guide you. I myself cannot risk it. These few mushrooms I've gathered are a small fraction of what we'll harvest. We need more. Indeed, we need to reach the source, deep below.

POET: But I tremble at the thought of an illuminable dungeon of pure darkness?

Alphonse ambles over to Poet. He caresses the pig's head.

POET: Alphonse...

LEATHER: He quite likes you both.

SEBASTIAN: Is that it?

LEATHER: No. One more thing.

Leather breaks some of the mushroom into pieces, and throws two clumps at both Sebastian and Poet.

LEATHER: I'd like you to eat them. I can't sacrifice anyone on the island. I need to see the fungal effects directly...

ELECTOR OF SALMON (bureaucratic composure regained): We'll call upon the island nurse in case something inauspicious happens.

POET: O, but what if we perish! I don't like mushrooms as it is.

SEBASTIAN: Yeah, perish... Or, I don't know. I have Crohn's disease, you see. Some people think it's like IBS, but it's much more inconvenient.

LEATHER: It is but a small sampling. I'm sure all will find it agreeable.

ELECTOR OF SALMON: Yes, you'll find it agreeable.

POET: I am averse to psychotic episodes. I prefer the rational flow of steadiness. I don't want to disappear.

SEBASTIAN: I'll do it. Yeah. Like your father famously said. Who cares. We'll have some of that.

LEATHER: May it act as manure on your field.

POET: I hold sympathy for the image.

SEBASTIAN: We have no choice.

Poet and Sebastian eat the mushrooms. Their effect is immediate.

Sebastian and Poet are inside the volcano coves. They do not know how they have arrived. They exist, for the time being, in a shared fugue-like daze. It is as if they are both inside the same dream, knowing the other is a mutual dreamer, clinging to a reality that exists only by consensus. This isn't really happening. Or it is, completely. The inside of the cove is, to their surprise, maintained and furnished: where one would expect flowstone and stalactite, there are powder blue walls, adorned with empty picture frames. Fine, intricate parquet on the ground. There are no doors or windows. There is a staircase which leads to a floor below. They are dressed as clowns: red, bulbous noses, face paint, billowing pants. Clown clothes. Something, or someone, is speaking through them.

POET: There ought to be clowns.

SEBASTIAN: Yes, there ought to be clowns.

POET: No one has to give us a reason. I think of the blood in my body dyed a deeper red. It is like a waterslide of clownhood.

SEBASTIAN: We must murder that pig. He is to blame. They will give us a prize.

POET: No, as clowns we must make the people laugh. Our audiences find it amusing.

SEBASTIAN: When we laugh, no one else laughs.

POET: I laugh once a year, maybe twice. It's a great joy.

SEBASTIAN: In my spare time I draw on napkins with cheap plastic pens, but even then I am filled with the murderous rage of a clown. My pants are soaked in seltzer water.

POET: We are making the world less lonely because of the great laughter we engender in our onlookers.

SEBASTIAN: It's our job and that's how it is.

POET: I love all kinds of seltzer: lemon-lime seltzer, peach seltzer, cherry seltzer.

SEBASTIAN: The other day I saw a new flavor: seedless watermelon.

They descend the stairs. The room below looks identical to the room before, except the dozen or so picture frames now display the portrait of a young woman, Clara.

POET: My lost sister! The rifle of my mind!

PORTRAITS OF CLARA (all portraits speaking at once): Enough. Too much of the orphan clown in you.

SEBASTIAN: (sneezes) I am indifferent to your household dramas and debacles. The susurrations of your family den speak.

POET: You would not like to see a clown who cries right in front of you, dear sister.

PORTRAITS OF CLARA: Shut it, clown orphan!

SEBASTIAN: (sneezes) I tend to cry in strange places. At the toilet for example. I'll have a bit of a cry there.

POET: The rifle of my mind, please shoot once for this old clown won't you?

SEBASTIAN: (seems like a sneeze; it's difficult to tell)

POET:

SEBASTIAN: (stiff)

POET: (sneezes)

They descend a staircase. Another identical room, picture frames now empty again. There is the statue at its center, one from Leather's. It's the statue that looks like it's masturbating.

POET: And what do we think about sex?

SEBASTIAN: God, please, let's not.

POET: What about men in shorts? They're often too long, no? Why even bother?

SEBASTIAN: We should send them to a country.

POET: And sucking lollipops?

SEBASTIAN (clown blood pouring from eyes): I'm in pain…

POET: We're both in pain. How could we not be in pain?

SEBASTIAN: This clown blood is getting everywhere.

POET: Our face practically says it: "We are clowns. We are pain."

SEBASTIAN: All four of my grandparents were clowns.

POET: I went to college for it.

SEBASTIAN: All eight of my great-grandparents were clowns.

POET: My parents were receptionists.

SEBASTIAN: My whole life, I've only seen one kind of shoe.

POET: Clown shoes.

SEBASTIAN: We just called them shoes.

They descend another staircase. This room has a tropical island theme. Coconuts litter the ground. Alphonse sits in a hammock tied between two palm trees. Next to him on a night table is a fruit-emblazoned cocktail he could not possibly drink. A miniature umbrella juts out from it.

ALPHONSE: Hello boys.

POET: (intimates throwing a pie)

SEBASTIAN: (intimates dying)

ALPHONSE: It's me, your friend Alphonse.

POET: (intimates writing a declaration of philosophical principles)

SEBASTIAN: (intimates burning)

There is a hole in the ground. Both throw themselves into the hole. They land on a large pile of gold coins inside what looks like a typical cave. The money is fake—a prop. A ring of torches illuminates the cavern. It smells of desiccated tiger corpses. Several of the island's everyday items appear and reappear in a continuous flow: socks, basketballs, a single Nintendo GameCube, self-help books, toilet paper, etc.

POET: The number of people I've spoken to increases every day.

SEBASTIAN: Clowns don't speak. We think about speaking.

POET: I smile at babies. I feel like the president.

SEBASTIAN: We're the presidents of laughter.

POET: No, we're the presidents of something else, but not laughter.

SEBASTIAN: We're the mayors of an abandoned sideshow amusement.

POET: Yes.

SEBASTIAN: We run the amusement. Its activities.

POET: Yes. Even if no one comes: there it is.

SEBASTIAN: There it is. The amusement. Someone should make a movie about us.

POET: Yes, a movie.

SEBASTIAN: A movie about hugging and all that.

POET: Hugging and smoothing things over with one's hand.

SEBASTIAN: No kissing.

POET: Never kissing.

SEBASTIAN: We only kiss pies and pie product.

POET: We ask very little of the world.

SEBASTIAN: The smallest amount one could ask for.

They slide down a fireman's pole through another hole in the ground. Dirt floor, no lights. It smells strongly of fungus.

POET: We have to tell the story eventually.

SEBASTIAN: But we could never tell a story.

POET: That's true.

SEBASTIAN: For clowns, there is only the present.

POET: Right. So we can't tell the story, even though we should.

SEBASTIAN: We should do a lot of things.

POET: But we won't. Or can't.

SEBASTIAN: We do clown things.

POET: That should be enough.

SEBASTIAN: I like clowns and clown-related matters.

POET: We can like.

SEBASTIAN: We can like well.

POET: I like waiting in line with several other angry clowns. It's work, but I like it.

SEBASTIAN: When we work, we play. When we don't work, we grieve.

POET: Every new thought is something new to think about.

SEBASTIAN: Each one feels more serious than the last.

POET: We're bad clowns when we aren't working.

SEBASTIAN: Everyone is a worse version of themselves when they aren't working. Even clowns.

POET: We're still human?

SEBASTIAN: We're plastic.

They march in darkness until they feel a doorknob. They open the door. It's a room with a farm theme. It's overly hot, and everything is made of plastic foam.

POET: (sneezes like a farm animal)

SEBASTIAN: (sneezes like a robber baron)

POET: (sneezes like a narrator)

SEBASTIAN: (sneezes like a narrator's friend)

They descend a staircase. It is the first room again. It also has a farm theme now. There's an EXIT sign above a door.

POET: This was my psycho-romp, please be kind.

SEBASTIAN: Yes, very nice to see you, too.

POET: We're your hosts for tonight. Applause.

SEBASTIAN: I hope you brought your allergy medication. Audience laughter.

POET: When did you first take up clowning?

SEBASTIAN: Oh, you know.

POET: What a coincidence.

SEBASTIAN: How do you figure. Stuff some pills into my mouth, won't you?

POET: We started clowning on the same day.

SEBASTIAN: I know.

POET: You know?

SEBASTIAN: I was there! We made this decision together.

POET: Ah, that's right.

SEBASTIAN: Always forgetting.

POET: A clown can't forget. We share one memory.

SEBASTIAN: There you have it, folks: clown memory!

POET: Clown cemetery.

SEBASTIAN: Clown theatre!

POET: Clown literature.

SEBASTIAN: Clown theory!

POET: Clowns on stage.

POET: Long night ahead.

SEBASTIAN: Yes. The parking lot of night.

POET: No. Night's empty parking lot. Except for clown cars.

SEBASTIAN: (sneezes)

They leave the room.

During their reverie, Poet and Sebastian have vanished and reappeared throughout various parts of the island. Unbeknownst to them, they have strangled Leather and Elector of SALMON to death. Alphonse escaped Leather's house and has since wandered the island. He now rests at the beach, staring off into the horizon. Sebastian and Poet have just reappeared next to him, on the edge of the water. Several hours have passed. It is dawn. Next to them, Golden Boy is fishing with his father. They both use ludicrously large fishing poles.

DRIVER: Here they are.

GOLDEN BOY: Are they back to normal?

DRIVER: We can hope!

POET: Normal?

GOLDEN BOY: You don't remember?

SEBASTIAN: No.

DRIVER: Throughout the night... Your eyes were white, total blanks, both of you carrying things. The statues from Leather's. You were throwing them into the ocean. Someone tried stopping you—Metallurgist Without Flute, I think—but you nearly beat him to death. We had to bring him to the island nurse.

GOLDEN BOY: One of you kept vanishing and the other would drag a statue on the ground and then that one would vanish. Then the first one would reappear and commence the dragging, and then the second one would reappear and you'd have an easier time of it... I thought of helping you even, but I didn't want to get involved. You threw our founder into the ocean. Deposited him there.

DRIVER: Good on you, son. Don't get involved with these non-islanders. No offense, lads. I never cared much for our founder to start with, really. We have a peaceful life here without him.

POET: Yes, none taken.

SEBASTIAN: None taken at all. I don't remember anything.

POET: Not a drop of memory. I am tired.

SEBASTIAN: Extremely tired. And hungry.

Driver takes out a loaf of German Schwartzbrot from his rucksack.

SEBASTIAN: Not the stately German black bread!

GOLDEN BOY: Oh, but much improved!

POET: I'll take it.

All have a chew. Sebastian transforms into a tiger.

POET: Oh.

GOLDEN BOY: Wait a tick. He's transformed into some kind of blasted cat thing.

Sebastian transforms back into Sebastian (normal version).

SEBASTIAN: What's happening to me?

POET: We must find a way to control the mushroom's hold on us. Yes, that's it! Control it.

SEBASTIAN: I don't know how.

POET: Think about transforming into a tiger again.

DRIVER: Maybe it's like meditation. Ground yourself. Focus on all your zones.

GOLDEN BOY: I'm not sure that's right.

DRIVER: I swear to you they put those instructions in a book.

Sebastian transforms into a tiger again. He cleans himself. Poet vanishes. He reappears a few feet away, at the top of a palm tree. He climbs down and returns to the shore. Golden Boy and Driver have been looking at Sebastian-Tiger silently. Alphonse seems unbothered by the confusion. Sebastian returns to normal once more.

POET: Have you been caring for our Alphonse?

GOLDEN BOY: I quite like him, it's true. Can we keep him father?

DRIVER: Certainly. A stout pig, with a comely dignity, I'd add.

SEBASTIAN: No complaints from us. You have our blessing.

Sebastian vanishes again. He reappears. He turns into a tiger and runs away. We do not hear from him again.

POET: Well, I'll be going now.

GOLDEN BOY: Where to, friend?

POET: I wanted to go to SALMON! But that was impossible. No, that's not possible for me any longer. And I have no reason to return home, it's true. Moreover, I cannot. For all that awaits me there is a life that is one day long. No tomorrows, more of the same today. My parents are likely dead, at the very least moribund. But I shall indeed be the author of my own life. With fungal assistance, I will embrace a certain atavist disposition, I believe. I cannot go to SALMON, so I am going to become a fish. Goodbye, Alphonse.

The pig oinks. Poet walks into the ocean. He becomes a fish. Swims away. The sun once again offers its apology down to the earth. Driver and Golden Boy cast their lines back into the water.

END.

ACKNOWLEDGEMENTS

I would like to thank Lucy K. Shaw, without whose generosity and kindness the publishing of this book would not be possible. I would also like to thank Kit Schluter for his wonderful illustrations and cover design. Additionally, I would like to thank Alex Rubert, Crow Jonah Norlander, Zac Smith, Giacomo Pope, and Robert Trevisan for their help, suggestions, encouragement, and friendship.

BIOGRAPHY

Sebastian Castillo is the author of Not I and
49 Venezuelan Novels. He lives in Philadelphia,
PA.

For the secret liner notes to this book, visit:

shabbydollhouse.com/salmonallcaps

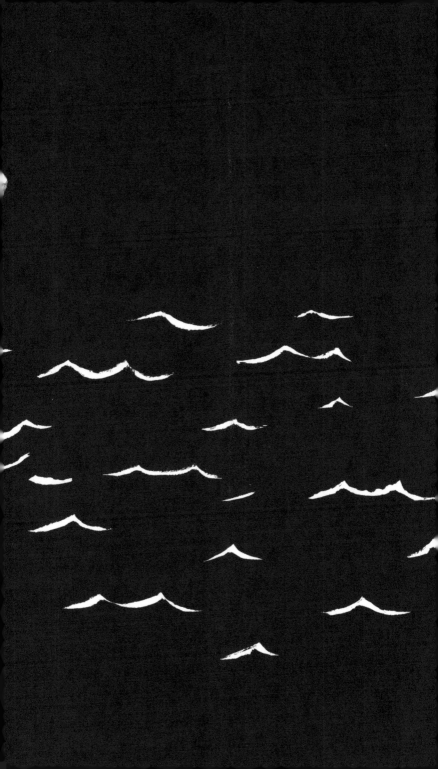

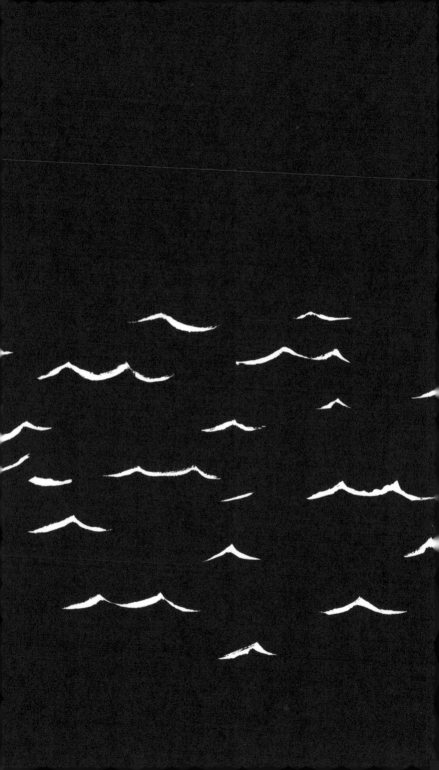